About the author

AF167707

Dr Keith Fisher has been a chemist all his working life. He was born in Birmingham in 1940, during the bombing. Passing the 11-plus allowed him to go to a grammar school in Smethwick.

Leaving school, he worked in chemical laboratories and did his degree, part-time. After graduation he went to Canada to start a post-graduate degree, which he finished at the University of London, gaining a Ph.D.

Post-doctoral studies and several teaching positions at universities in America took up the next five years. Following his return to the UK, he took up a senior lectureship at the University of Lagos, followed by a post at the University of Khartoum. After nearly thirteen years in Africa, he spent two years in Canada before coming to Australia in 1989.

His Uncle Percy was a great story teller and this is what stirred the author's interest in short stories.

TWO BRUMMIES OUT IN THE WORLD

Keith Fisher

TWO BRUMMIES OUT IN THE WORLD

Vanguard Press

A CIP catalogue record for this title is
available from the British Library.

ISBN 978-1-80016-384 3

*Vanguard Press is an imprint of
Pegasus Elliot MacKenzie Publishers Ltd.*
www.pegasuspublishers.com

First Published in 2022

**Vanguard Press
Sheraton House Castle Park
Cambridge England**

Printed & Bound in Great Britain

Dedication

To my first wife, Janet; my children, Teresa, Alex and Sarah, who have all lived in Africa. Teresa has lived in Tanzania for nearly thirty years (my fault).

To my second wife, Ela, who has lived in Africa and now lives with me in Australia.

Acknowledgements

Thanks to my North American friends, Tony Homer (USA) and Midge Dean (Canada), for useful corrections and hints.

A Brummie (Birmingham) lad in Africa

Ari, everybody called him Harry, lived in Ladywood in Birmingham. His parents owned a paper shop in the area. They were Jewish but not religious, they did not go to the synagogue and Ari was brought up without religion. At school the teachers tried to get him to go to Sunday school but his parents always arranged an outing on Sunday afternoon, many of his friends were envious of his ability to miss Sunday school. Ari took no interest in religion, even when he was told Jesus was a Jew.

Ladywood was a very working-class suburb and the area had been described as a Victorian slum. As a young boy, Ari did not notice any problems with the area. He used to play in the street with all the other kids. Marbles, hopscotch and French cricket were his favourites when he was small. Then it was football, as he became older. Football could get aggressive and often there were fights over a simple problem or dispute and Ari learnt how to defend himself. His father was quite strict and wouldn't let Ari leave the local area. As a treat, he could go to the Regent cinema in Ledsom Street (often called the Flea Pit) but not to any other cinemas in the area. When Ari was fifteen, he treated himself to a show at the Crown Cinema in Icknield Port Road, within easy walking distance.

No one in Ari's street, had a car, when his father bought a Ford Prefect, everyone was in awe. His dad was a friendly bloke and everyone in the area liked him. Ari's mother was always giving sweets to the local children, many mothers would come to thank her and seek personal advice. This was a rough but generally friendly neighbourhood.

Early in the 1930s, there were rumblings of war but no one in this neighbourhood took much notice. Ari watched his father listening to the radio news every night but he also took no interest. Ari liked the music and comedy shows on the radio but not the news. His fourteenth birthday in 1934 was celebrated with a big cake and a party for his friends. Many of his friends never had cake and it was soon devoured. After 1934, things started to change. Ari's family were visited by a few relatives from Germany, who generally stayed only one or two days and then moved on. Ari learnt a few German phrases and met a couple of very good-looking girls, unfortunately, they did not stay long. Attitudes of some of the locals started to change. There seemed to be more political arguments in the street. There were a few people in the area talking badly about Jews and Yids. Ari asked his father, "What is a Yid?"

"Some people speak Yiddish, which is like a dialect of German and Hebrew but I think you shouldn't say Yid. It's a bad word. Try to ignore these people."

Although Ari's father did not forbid the word, Ari decided he would never say it again. Whenever he heard the word, he would ignore the speaker. As the years passed, Ari noticed more street arguments and when Oswald Mosely came to Birmingham, things became a bit tense. Ari's father asked him to stay in — or close to — the shop.

The relatives coming from Germany and Poland had some dreadful stories and Ari's father started to see an adverse effect on his son. Ari had left school at fifteen and was working in the paper shop. Some people entering the shop would say bad things about Jews and it made him angry. He was hearing these dreadful stories from Europe and he wanted to speak out, but his father recommended caution.

Ari was spending some time at a part-time college in Birmingham and doing very well in maths and science. His father let him have one day a week to go to college and he was spending two nights a week doing a variety of courses. He enjoyed college as he was getting bored in the shop. At college he had met an African from the Gold Coast. They struck up a friendship and Ari dreamed of travel. His friend told him about Africa with its chiefs, peculiar customs and about thatched huts in villages with no paved roads.

Ali's parents decided he should go abroad as they could see problems for him if the war came, and it looked like coming. One night Ari sat down to dinner with his father and mother and they asked him if he would like to travel.

"Yes, please. I've never even been to Scotland."

"Where would you like to go?"

"Africa."

"Well, we have cousins in South Africa, Nigeria and the Sudan and any of them would be glad to take on a strong lad to help in their business. There are some problems in South Africa, we don't like their racial policies, Nigeria is hot and humid and Khartoum, in the Sudan, is in the middle of the desert. Your choice, but we would prefer you not to choose South Africa, although you might do better there."

"I need to talk to a friend and go to the library and consult some atlases. Now you have mentioned South Africa, Nigeria and Sudan, I have something to look at."

His African friend said that Lagos was a rough city but a place to make money. He knew nothing of the other countries. The library was within walking distance, on the edge of Ladywood, so Ari spent many an evening there. He met an old soldier, called Tom, in the library. Tom had been in Egypt and had fought alongside some Sudanese, whom he described as beautiful people and good soldiers, trained in Khartoum by British officers and Sergeant Majors. Their English was poor but they were very friendly.

Cairo was generally dry and even though it was hot it was bearable, unless it rained. Khartoum would be hotter but drier and it rarely rained. Together, they pored over maps and Ari had no choice but to pick Khartoum. Tom picked out Port Sudan and then Ari could go across the desert to Khartoum. Ari was excited about travelling across the desert. He really had no comprehension of the desert, he thought it was a load of sand.

His parents had already noted his intention and had written to their cousin. They wanted him to leave England before his eighteenth birthday. They feared that there would be some kind of conscription and that boys from poor areas would be picked first.

Ari had started to move around Birmingham and realised that Ladywood wasn't the best part of the city. When he decided to leave, he thought about what he would miss. At his age he was a very sensible lad but even then, the spirit of adventure was overriding his other senses. He would miss his mates but not the climate; he would miss his parents but not some of the older people in the street who had started to swear at him. The library was now his favourite place and he would miss the old soldier, his first old friend. He would miss riding on a tram.

Within a month, a letter arrived from his Uncle Jacob in Khartoum, welcoming Ari to join the company. Jacob was Ari's father's cousin, but should be called uncle. He was a widower with no children and had lived in Khartoum for at least twenty years. He was a trader living in a trading city, Khartoum was at a crossroads for many trading routes and many nationalities lived there, passing on goods to the east, west, north and south. Ari would help organise the company and because of his English, he would be in charge of introducing new customers. Of course, being a strong young lad, he could take some of the physical burden from his uncle.

Ari was excited and told his old friend in the library how he couldn't wait to leave. His old mate cautioned him and warned him of sea sickness, home sickness and the heat. Physical work in a hot climate could be very difficult and the need to consume water was very important. Tom warned him that he would have to learn Arabic, as English may be understood by only a few Sudanese. As the time approached for his leaving, Ari could talk of nothing else, so his father sat him down for a reality check.

"You are going to Khartoum to work; you'll need a bit of enjoyment but not too much. Your Uncle Jacob has invited other young relatives to work with him but they have preferred to go to America, South America or South Africa. He's getting old but he's still in charge, do not try to override him. Your journey will be interesting but try to learn things as you go and not treat it as a holiday. Working conditions will be difficult as the temperature is often over a hundred degrees Fahrenheit, take things easy. We'll miss you but we think this is a great opportunity. I think it will be many years before we meet again."

That last statement had an effect and the old soldier's talk about homesickness had also sunk in, but

Ari was young and there was plenty of time to come home. Now his friends started to get a bit bored with Ari's coming adventure, they were going nowhere soon. Little did they know. Many of his friends were envious but they did not want to show it.

A passage was booked on a freighter leaving Liverpool. Ari would disembark from the ship at Port Sudan. The paper shop had to be shut on a Wednesday so that Ari could be taken to Liverpool by car. Ari's mother wanted to see him off and much to Ari's father's regret, they had to lose a day of earning money. A few of his friends came to wish him goodbye and even though it was early morning, it seemed that half the street's residents were waving at the car. The road to Liverpool seemed to be long but it was all new to Ari; it was also new to his father. Ari's father and mother had arrived from Germany and had landed in London. They took the train to Birmingham and Ari's father had never driven outside Birmingham. He had several maps but he was a bit apprehensive, taking on a long drive.

Ari's father was becoming a bit worried after getting lost a couple of times. Finally, they stopped and asked directions. They were, in fact, on the correct road and they finally arrived at the dock area. There were several ships in port, they all looked huge to Ari and he was excited. The dock area had some forbidding signs and it took a while before Ari found out where to go. There were customs and immigration checks, before he could enter the dock area. Ari's passport was a few years old and unused, the family had planned to visit relatives in France but that journey had fallen through. The immigration officer smiled as he looked at the youthful photo inside but did not cause a problem. Ari's mother was in tears as he entered the dock, but his father gave him a stern warning that he should behave himself and write regularly.

Ari wandered along the dock until he found his ship, which was one of the smallest vessels but still huge. His luggage consisting of one small suitcase was no burden but as he ascended the gangplank, a seaman relieved him of his bag and Ari was then shown to the upper deck to meet the captain. Ari was in a bit of a trance and overawed at meeting the captain. He had expected him to be English but instead, he was Egyptian. The captain wanted to meet a paying passenger who was going to Sudan, explaining that this was a cargo ship that would stop at many ports to offload and onload goods. Most of their trade would be along the East African coast and they would be going through the Suez Canal. This excited Ari even more, as his old mate had told him about the canal. The captain explained that Ari would have to share a cabin with the navigator, an Irishman. They had planned to leave today but were awaiting more cargo and would probably leave tomorrow, at this rate.

Ari suddenly realised he had forgotten to wave to his parents but when he returned to the deck, they had gone. He explored the ship for a while, although it seemed huge there were very few places to go. The navigator was a very talkative Irishman but he did outline their voyage and the possible problem areas. They would sail south from Liverpool and enter the English Channel and that could be rough. They would then head across to the Bay of Biscay (which could also be rough). The ship might stop at Oporto, depending on the cargo, and then head south to Gibraltar. Ari had heard a lot about Gibraltar as some of his relatives had escaped from Spain via the island. The Irishman explained that, even in Gibraltar, they may not be able to leave the ship. Ari was shown to his cabin and it amused him that the walls were made of steel.

Ari noticed how well the Egyptian captain had spoken English. He also noticed how the Irishman made his English sound like a song. He now started to realise his own English was different, he had a pronounced Birmingham accent.

When the ship set out from Liverpool, Ari had a strange feeling, it was as though he was losing something. That emotion was only temporary, as his adventure was just beginning. The cabin was small with a porthole, a wash basin and two bunk beds. Ari had the top bunk with a ladder. He was to spend a good time in that bunk as the weather turned bad. The bed and he would go up and then he would meet the bed, as it was coming up again. Up on the deck wasn't much better, as the wind was cold and the spray blinding. In the wheel house, it was much calmer but he was a bit annoyed at the sniggers of the crew seeing his discomfort.

Patrick (everybody called him Paddy) was the only person who really talked to Ari. The captain was too busy and the crew did not understand him and he did not understand them. The Italian cook was okay but a conversation with him was like pulling teeth. Ari spent most days staring out to sea, watching the horizon and realising how big the sea was compared to the land. He went down to the engine room but did not stay long. He learnt not to be a stoker, it was too bloody hot. Paddy told him he might suffer from claustrophobia — a new word to Ari. Being with Paddy meant that he could learn how to read maps, which were far more detailed than the ones in the library. Ari had a fascination for maps, some of them had so much detail that Paddy had to explain some of the features.

They did not stop at Oporto as there was no significant cargo to take on board. Paddy said they would stop at Gibraltar and that would be a great sight, he had been on this trip several times but had never landed there. This trip wasn't going to change his record. As they approached Gibraltar, Ari was witnessing a most fantastic sight. He couldn't take his eyes off the hill/mountain in front of him. He had seen nothing like it before but then, he had seen very few spectacular sights. The harbour had many buildings but everything was overshadowed by this huge rock. There seemed to be a road to the top, where there was a flagpole, but the sheer size of the place had Ari mesmerised. There were only small hills around Birmingham.

As they docked, he noticed soldiers everywhere. The captain explained that there was a military exercise taking place and they would pick up their goods and be on their way. Ari was disappointed, he would have liked to explore the town, which seemed to surround the base of the rock. Only the captain was allowed to leave the ship to talk to the agent.

As the ship wandered along the French coast, there seemed to be a similar story at each port, offload, onload and go. Ari was still enjoying the sights. Each port seemed to be different and Paddy pointed out some of the interesting features. Ari was thinking he had visited France without actually stepping foot on land. Paddy was reassuring, and said that when they arrived at Alexandria, they would have some shore leave. He showed Ari their route on the map.

Ari couldn't wait until they arrived in Egypt but as they docked, this seemed to be a different kind of port. This place was teeming with people and whereas other ports had seemed to be organised, this was chaos. There were lots of buildings of all sizes and several mosques, which Paddy pointed out, calling them Islamic churches. He laughed when Ari spoke of his misgivings, they could get lost in this crowd.

"This is very efficient port. They want what you have to offer, and they want you to take what they have to offer. Egyptians want transactions to be done as quickly as possible. Alex is an interesting place we'll explore together. Don't worry — I've been here before."

The captain said they would spend two nights in port and everyone should beware of the temptations available. Ari asked Paddy what he meant.

"Number one, the brothels and the girls; number two, the drugs, such as cocaine and heroin; and number three, fathers and brothers with shotguns. Maybe one and three are similar. Number four is very strong liquor, which could render you unconscious."

"Well, I'm not looking for a girl; I don't know anything about drugs and I don't drink. I think I'm safe," smiled Ari.

"Yes, but you are still a teenager."

Ari watched the crew off-loading cargo and a multitude of porters carrying sacks away, on their heads. Paddy came up and assured Ari that everything was organised and nothing would get lost unless they did. They descended the gangway on to the dock and the crew were smiling and waving at them.

"What are they saying?" Ari asked, looking back.

"They are basically saying not to get lost or robbed. You ought to learn a bit of Arabic, you'll need it in the Sudan."

As Paddy and Ari wandered through the market near the dock, Ari was astounded by the noise. He had been on a ship where the engines had a sort of throbbing rhythm and the wind and the waves were steady, but this was human noise at a high pitch. Paddy explained that each stall had something to sell and the owners were shouting out their wares and prices. Birmingham market was quiet compared to this one. As Paddy was explaining the noise, he suddenly stopped.

"We're being followed, just follow me into this café and don't look round," he said, in a low voice.

The café was little more than an awning with two crude tables and four crude chairs with rope seats. They sat and ordered two coffees. Ari had never drunk coffee, his father had said he was too young. Paddy explained that three men had been following them and they were standing across the street.

"Why are they following us?"

"Because they think we're rich. We're foreigners."

"Well, I'm not rich and I think we could fight them. They look skinny."

"They probably have knives and we don't want a problem with the local police. The last thing we want is for the captain to have to bail us out of prison."

Ari and Paddy sat drinking their coffee. It was strong and with no milk; only sugar, Ari thought it bitter. Luckily, Mario, the ship's cook, came walking towards them.

"Mario — come and sit and have a coffee. We have a problem."

Paddy explained to Mario that they were being followed and these men might have knives. Mario reached into his pocket and pulled out a flick knife. The men across the street saw it and moved on.

Mario smiled. "In many ports, I take out my knife to clean it or clean my fingernails. I do it openly so those around me can see, I have no problems. The big problem is pick-pockets. They would like to get my knife."

Ari hated to waste anything but decided his coffee was too bitter. He offered it to Mario but he declined. They all decided they had seen enough of the market and headed back to the ship. Ari was still bemused as to why anyone would think him rich. Paddy explained there were many pointers, the colour of his skin; his clothes; and the mode of his speech. Paddy and Mario both agreed that few locals would understand what Ari said and they both laughed.

"Is my English not good enough?"

"Let us say that you use English in a different way," said Paddy, being polite.

Ari was still thinking about their experience. He had wanted to look into the shops but their visit had been rudely curtailed. The captain was glad to see them back as he wanted to leave Alexandria, having heard there might be some problem in the port as dock workers were claiming they had not been paid. There were also some rumblings from Italy, where Mussolini was in charge, in addition to a rumour that Palestine was to be partitioned. The captain wanted to get through the Suez Canal before any real problem started. Being Egyptian, he was well informed of the local news.

Everyone was aboard and within two hours the ship left the port. The captain explained to the crew that, normally, he would try to pick up cargo at other ports but he was keen to get south of any future problems. They wouldn't be docking at any Egyptian ports. The crew liked this captain, he explained things.

The captain took Paddy and Ari aside and said they wouldn't be docking at Port Said and the next stop would be Port Sudan. Paddy was to plot a course avoiding all Egyptian ports, the captain felt there was some trouble brewing. He thought that there would be demonstrations at other ports and this provided the opportunity to lose cargo off the dock.

Ari enjoyed the next few days as Paddy and he pored over maps. These were all British Navy maps and had a lot of detail. It reminded Ari of his time in the library with the old soldier. As they passed through Port Said, Ari was to see the next great wonder, the Suez Canal. Paddy explained the workings of the canal and Ari couldn't get over the sheer size. At some places, they were passing huge ships just metres apart. A couple of times, he held his breath. This was so exciting and whereas the Rock of Gibraltar had been magnificent, this was exhilarating. When they entered Suez and left the canal, Ari was almost sad, he wanted to do that again. In contrast, the captain was relieved.

As they sailed down the Red Sea, Paddy explained there were coral reefs — dangerous to shipping but very beautiful for swimmers. Ari had never thought of underwater dangers for shipping. They were sailing almost out of sight of land and they had to be careful. Ari was learning a lot from Paddy. The captain was also now friendlier and Ari was going to eat at the captain's table, whereas previously he had eaten with the crew. He thought the crew food was different and tasty. Paddy instructed Ari on the use of the cutlery and the wine glasses. The small sherry glass would come at the end of the meal. Ari had never drunk wine and certainly not sherry, but he wanted to try anything. He felt proud that the captain had invited him to dinner.

Mario saluted Ari as he approached the captain's table and Paddy showed him to his seat next to the captain. Ari had rarely spoken to the captain but now he was going to have to say at least a few words. Ari thought he should thank the captain and start the conversation.

"Thank you, sir. I understand that my English is a bit different and I hope you can understand me."

"You have a dialect that I find difficult but when I read Shakespeare, I see that you are speaking close to his language. When I get home, I'm going to confuse my family by speaking like you. You have taught me something new."

"Where is your family, sir?"

"They currently live in Crete and I would have liked to pass by the island, but I fear there is going to be a problem in the region and I have an obligation to the ship owners to continue to trade."

The first course came and it was a choice between soup or stuffed olive leaves. Paddy suggested trying the stuffed olive leaves. They were delicious. They had meat and rice in the leaves and some kind of sauce that left Ari wanting more. The next course had a choice, there was chicken with pasta, or red capsicum stuffed with minced lamb, olives and okra. Ari had never heard of okra but Paddy advised he try that dish. The captain warned it could be a bit peppery but Ari had eaten a few of his mother's dishes with pepper. Paddy realised that Mario was doing his best for Ari. Ari loved this meal, it was all so tasty. He was hoping he could get some of this food in Khartoum.

The captain poured Ari some red wine and said it came from Cyprus. The wine was semi-sweet but Ari's first taste suggested it was a bit sour. Paddy advised that the next sips would be more palatable and not to upset the captain by saying he did not like the wine. As he ate the lamb, the wine started to taste better and by the time he finished the lamb he was enjoying it. Now for the sweet! Mario had made a Dundee Cake and covered it with a brandy sauce (lots of brandy); he topped it with whipped cream and had, somewhere, found a strawberry for the pinnacle. Ari thought it was too good to eat but the captain insisted that Ari cut a piece that included the strawberry.

When the sherry came, Ari was feeling very full. The captain explained that Ari had been a very good paying passenger (they did not get many). He had been good with the crew and his English had renewed the captain's interest in Shakespeare. He wished him well in Sudan and hoped they would meet again. Ari's first taste of sherry was a bit surprising but the first toast was followed by more. By this time, he was feeling a bit light-headed.

The captain advised Ari that he would need to know a few basic Arab words as he assumed that in Port Sudan, no one would speak English.

"I have been learning some words from the crew."

The captain rolled his eyes. "I hope they are decent words."

Paddy nodded agreement — he had already vetted some of the words. With Ari's accent, Paddy thought he might have problem with Arabic words but Ari could copy the sounds and remember them. He now had a very basic vocabulary.

Paddy suggested that he write a letter to his parents as there would be many ships passing Port Sudan that carried mail. Arriving at Port Sudan, Ari packed his meagre possessions into his small suitcase and looked around the cabin, he would miss it. Sometimes, at night, he had felt the cabin was closing in on him but became used to being calm in the cabin. He was loathe to leave the ship. He had learned many things on this trip, and the ship had been his home for a while. Paddy and Mario were at the end of the gangplank to wish him well and even the captain came over to say that he hoped Khartoum would see Ari make his fortune.

Ari was now alone. Within seconds he was missing his friends but he had to find his relative in Khartoum. He looked around. This was a small port, almost silent. The buildings around looked very poor and almost deserted. A man holding a crude cardboard sign with Ari's name printed in poor English approached him. Ari was relieved that someone was meeting him. They looked at each other and Ari said "Khartoum?"

"Yes, sah. Me Abdul — you Ari?"

Abdul directed Ari to the most ancient and dilapidated lorry. Abdul backed the lorry up to the dock and picked up several cases with the help of the dockers. This loading was all done by hand and Ari resisted the temptation to help, as it was very hot and sticky. He was starting to miss the cooling sea breeze. Ari looked around the lorry, it was so old. The front windscreen had a crack on the driver's side. The passenger side window looked intact. The doors had no windows and looked as if they were about to fall off. There were no real seats — just a mattress across the cabin; at least that was comfortable. Ari wandered around the lorry, seeing dents everywhere. The back had obviously been hit several times. Only one back light was intact. One front light had a cracked glass and the bumper bar had several dents.

After the lorry had been loaded, Abdul jumped into the cabin and placed a large knife between Ari and himself.

"*Harami*. Bad men."

"I know that word — it means robbers."

Abdul shook his head in agreement. "*Yallah.*"

Ari wasn't sure what to say, so he just smiled. There were no paved roads in Port Sudan and when they left the town, there were just dirt tracks which soon petered out into sand. There was no conversation and all Ari could see was endless desert with almost no vegetation. He started to think about the drive from Birmingham to Liverpool, and how different the scenery was. There were neat hedgerows and green fields. The road was smooth with tarmac and now he was being bounced around with no road in sight. Paddy had put Ari's parents in his mind by making him write a letter, now he had time, and couldn't stop thinking of them.

After a few hours' drive, Abdul pulled over and produced a little stove. He motioned to Ari to sit in the shade of the lorry. As he sat by the vehicle, he looked around. The land wasn't all sand. There were plenty of rocky patches, not like the pictures he had seen in books. There seemed to be no vegetation, but then he spotted a small, green plant growing out of the sand. There was no other vegetation around. Ari let the warm sand filter through his hands.

Abdul boiled water and made tea. Ari had never had tea without milk and he watched Abdul put so much sugar in his tea, it couldn't all dissolve. Ari found the tea refreshing and then Abdul produced a large container of water. Now Ari realised how thirsty he was, and consumed several glasses of water before Abdul put up his hand, motioning him to stop. After a few more hours, some mud buildings appeared in the distance and as they approached them, there were a couple of houses. There were also a couple of trees and several goats. In the middle of this small village was a small well and some cultivated plots. Abdul motioned that they would eat and Ari now realised how hungry he was.

As they approached one house, a man came out and seeing Ari, he started to bow. They stopped there and the man offered a crude seat in the shade. Ari sat while Abdul entered the house and came out with two dishes, two large pieces of flat bread and a big container of water. Ari then noticed Abdul give the man a small bag of tea and a bag of sugar. The dish contained beans with half an egg and half a tomato. Abdul tore off a piece of bread and scooped up some of the beans, gesturing to Ari to do likewise. Ari was obviously not going to get a spoon or fork, so he copied Abdul. The beans were spicy but delicious and the water was cool, but not cold, and very welcome.

Ari pointed at the bread. "*Hubz*?"

Abdul nodded but said, "*Sudani — esh, hubz,* also good."

Ari thought to himself that they spoke Arabic in the Sudan, but this new word was a bit of a puzzle. He would have to ask his uncle. After eating, they left with lots of well-wishing and Ari even noticed a woman in the doorway, waving at them. These houses were so crude Ari wondered how they survived the howling wind in the desert, Tom had told him about desert winds. Abdul was happy but as they drove, it started to get dark. In fact, it became dark very quickly. The headlights of the lorry only showed the desert twenty feet in front and Ari was wondering how Abdul was navigating. Ari started to realise it was getting quite cool, ever since the sun went down, the temperature had dropped rapidly. Ari found a blanket behind his seat and Abdul smiled and nodded approval.

In the distance, Ari saw what he thought was a light that seemed to come and go as the track dipped and rose. Finally, he could see a light properly and as they came closer, it turned out to be another small village. There seemed to be a large fire and men standing around, roasting a goat. Abdul stopped the lorry and they were greeted by the villagers. They sat with the men. The women were not to be seen but as the goat was carved, he saw a young boy taking pieces of meat to one of the mud huts. The meat was tasty, if a little bit tough. Ari did not know that this was an old goat near to death and that it was killed and cooked within one hour. The villagers would never kill a fit goat. To wash the food down, Ari was given a couple of glasses of *aragi*, an alcoholic drink made from dates. The drink certainly helped him sleep.

The next day, they set out and Ari noticed an increase in vegetation and more villages. Abdul seemed increasingly excited and kept saying "Khartoum." Ari saw that the villages were getting bigger and the village where they stopped for lunch had a mosque. They were also able to pick up fuel for the lorry. There was no petrol station; just a place with barrels of diesel and petrol. Ari watched in amusement at the palaver to get fuel into the lorry. There was a crowd, all shouting and laughing, but only two men did the job. They siphoned the petrol from the drum and they called it benzene. This time, Abdul pulled out some notes to pay for the fuel.

After lunch, they set off again. The track was much smoother and there was some vegetation by the side of the road. Late in the afternoon, Ari could see lights on the horizon. He pointed to them.

"Khartoum?"

Abdul nodded his head in a negative sense and said, "Kassala."

Ari had not realised they were still many miles from Khartoum but the road was going to get better. They stayed overnight in Kassala and feasted on fried liver with beans, tomatoes, dates and of course, unleavened bread. They also had a couple of glasses of aragi and Ari enjoyed another good sleep.

The next day they travelled along an unpaved road but it was fairly smooth. Ari saw a few lorries and two cars — the first cars he had seen in Sudan. Approaching the outskirts of Khartoum, there was much more vegetation and many more people. Abdul was reciting something Ari did not understand but he was doing it in a very excited way.

Khartoum

They pulled into the souk and stopped in front of a shop. There was a strong smell Ari couldn't place. Abdul explained they were roasting and grinding coffee beans two doors down the street. Out came an older man with a large black beard and a shawl around his shoulders. Ari thought this must be Uncle Jacob, as he was of similar stature to his father and the only real difference was a bigger, blacker beard. Ari jumped from the lorry and hugged his uncle. Jacob did not seem so enthusiastic but in a very heavy German accent, he said "Welcome."

Ari was looking at the shop as Jacob was greeting Abdul, he had the impression that this was a warmer greeting. Abdul had done all the hard work and brought the lorry and contents safely to Khartoum, so maybe he deserved a better welcome. While Abdul supervised the unloading of the lorry, Jacob ushered Ari into the shop. In all the excitement, Ari had not noticed the heat but when he entered the shop, he enjoyed the lower temperature.

"Why is it so cool in the shop?" he asked.

"We are using air coolers, where water is drawn across straw and a fan draws air through the straw."

Jacob's accent was quite strong and Ari had to digest the words but the meaning was clear. He looked around the shop and compared the chaotic display with his father's neat shop. This shop seemed to have everything, food stuffs, textiles, agricultural implements, mechanical tools yet none of it seemed to be in any order.

Jacob ushered Ari into a back room and made him sit at a table. He offered Ari a glass of water and then started to speak.

"I came to Khartoum many years ago and took a camel train from Port Sudan to Khartoum. The first thing I appreciated was water and the second thing was shade. It took over a week to get to Khartoum, where there was a golden opportunity, this is a trading town at the centre of many trade routes. In two years, I had a good business and sent for my wife. We met in Port Sudan where I lingered too long. She contracted malaria. On the road to Khartoum, it became worse and when we reached Khartoum, she died. I can't forgive myself and have lived alone ever since. I do not like to go to Port Sudan; I leave that to Abdul. There is a Jewish community here but I mix very little with them. My only real friend here is Abdul, he is indispensable to my business. None of my relatives are interested in helping me and you are the first to offer any help. If you stay and work hard, this will be yours when I'm gone."

Ari sat in silence and the last phrase caught his attention. He had not thought about owning anything, he was here to work. He was thinking, could he work in this heat?

"I'll try to do anything you ask, Uncle. I see this shop looks like a thriving enterprise." He was trying to find the correct words as he realised that Jacob might have a problem with his mode of speech.

Jacob then pulled out a bottle of wine and produced two glasses. "Let us toast to a prosperous venture. The first thing you must do is learn some local Arabic and reorganise this shop. You start tomorrow."

Ari wasn't expecting wine, it was sweet wine and he had become to enjoy a drier taste.

"Yes, Uncle. I've found that some Arabic words I know are different in Sudan."

"Some local words will be different but the basic language is the same. Many of the words Sudanese and Egyptians use will be different from other Arab countries. It's important to learn the local words, classical Arabic can wait till later."

The next morning Ari awoke at around dawn, having enjoyed a good sleep. He entered the shop to find it open with Abdul sitting behind the desk, he was obviously going to be the instructor. Ari pointed at a jar and said "English, honey."

"Sudani, *asal nahal*," replied Abdul.

"English, tea."

"Sudani, *chai.*"

"We call it tay."

Abdul looked quizzically at Ari.

"Never mind," Ari smiled.

This process went on for a while until the first customer arrived. He immediately went to Abdul but was directed to Ari. The customer looked bemused but in his best English said "Foul beans, please."

Abdul directed Ari to a sack of beans but Ari did not know how much to weigh out.

"How much?"

The customer looked bemused until Abdul said "*Beycam da?*"

"*Wahed* pound."

Now the English and Arabic were getting mixed up and Abdul had to tell Ari, "One pound."

This went on the whole morning and Ari memorised the counting system. He noticed only men came into the shop; very different to Ladywood. Later in the day, Jacob came to report that he had been off-selling some of the stock that arrived yesterday and had made a good profit. Jacob said that Abdul could have a rest and he would take over. There was no rest for Ari. At the end of the day, he was exhausted.

That evening they sat at the table, Jacob explaining his life in Khartoum and how he had met Abdul. He had bought an old van and taught Abdul how to drive. Abdul had found their present lorry and would follow the camel train to Port Sudan. Abdul soon memorised the route, bringing merchandise from Port Sudan was very profitable. Khartoum received goods from east, west, north and south. The next day Abdul would go to

Omdurman, where the camel trains came from the west, even as far as Morocco, and the south, as far as Nigeria. Abdul was indispensable to the business, he could always find bargains and he had an eye for what would sell in Khartoum.

Jacob opened another bottle of wine, saying he enjoyed wine but Abdul did not drink alcohol and this was the first time for years he had someone with whom to drink. Wine wasn't popular in Khartoum but he always had a supply from Ethiopia and occasionally received wine from France. There were a few Italians and Egyptians who bought wine but he had no Sudanese customers. Ari now enjoyed wine, too. He told Jacob about his trip. Jacob asked what cargo the ship was carrying and Ari had to admit he did not know. Jacob's reply was that any information was important, particularly when some of the products could be sold in Khartoum.

Jacob talked a lot about his time in Khartoum but not about his family; not even his wife. Ari began to wonder why Jacob never mentioned Ari's parents. He did not stop Jacob's stories but started to think about his parents and was now beginning to miss his home. Ari asked Jacob if there was a post office, as he wanted to write his parents a letter. This seemed to please Jacob and he said there might be mail sent by planes. He would enquire.

Ari's first Friday was a surprise. He awoke at dawn and went to the shop. Jacob was there alone and Ari asked about Abdul.

"Today is *Jumah*, the day of prayer. If you go outside, you'll see men praying. We don't get much trade today. I'm surprised you slept through the Imam calling the faithful to prayer at four a.m. The call from the minaret always seems louder on a Friday."

Ari looked outside to see men on their knees praying, even in the roadway. He started to wonder when Jacob slept. Ari spent most of his time tidying the shop and the back store, rather than rearranging the stock. During his clean-up, he found some old motors and pumps in the back of the store. The store was also full of old tools. When he asked his uncle if he could look at the motors, Jacob suddenly became excited.

"If you can fix those motors or pumps, my son, we have a new enterprise."

Jacob explained that these were air-cooler motors and pumps and they were often breaking down. The company that imported the water coolers couldn't fix any broken parts and you had to buy new parts. Khartoum was littered with broken parts. Ari had spent time at the Birmingham Institute and one of the courses was on electric motors. He now found some usable tools in the back room and started to take some of the motors apart. Some of the motors were completely burnt out but there were useful parts he could salvage from even the worst of them. He set up a rig in the store and when he started the first motor, Jacob was dancing a jig. Ari's next challenge was the water pumps and he found that most of them were clogged with sand. He constructed his own cooler and it worked.

In the meantime, Jacob spent more time in the shop and Ari more time in the backroom. Ari was quick to point out that his Arabic wasn't improving as he wasn't dealing with customers. Jacob was starting to appreciate the young man's worth and so he let Ari fix motors in the shop.

Ari said he would like to go to Port Sudan with Abdul to check out the ships and their cargo. He was secretly hoping to see Paddy and Mario but he said he could develop his Arabic with Abdul. Jacob thought that was a good idea but he was also keen on the cooler motors being sold. Ari explained that they and the problems were not going away but knowing what could be sold in Khartoum was important.

"My son, you are thinking like a trader, I like it."

The journey to Port Sudan was enjoyable now Ari knew what to expect. Abdul and he largely chatted in Arabic, Ari was picking up the language quite fast and Abdul's English was improving. In Port Sudan he did not meet up with Paddy and Mario but was able to get a list of the ships docking in the port. He was also able to get some idea of unassigned cargo that might be bought for cash. Abdul was very impressed, as he was always keen to visit Port Sudan.

Back in Khartoum, Jacob was also impressed, this young man had a trader's instinct. One day, an English officer entered the shop to buy some cloth. He was a bit taken aback by the sight of Ari fixing a motor. There was no one else in the shop.

"Do you speak English?" he asked.

"Well, if you understand my Brummie twang — yes."

"You're English and from Birmingham? What are you doing here?"

For the next ten minutes, Ari told his story, he was so glad to get it off his chest. This was the first English person he had met and this officer was from Warwick. The officer was in charge of the stores and acquisitions for the garrison, which was mainly training Sudanese soldiers.

"What are you doing with those motors?"

"These are water-cooler motors and I'm fixing the ones I can. I'm also fixing the water pumps."

"My god, you are just what we need. We rely on water coolers and when one breaks down, we have to wait forever for a new part. The British army doesn't understand water coolers. We have lots of broken motors and water pumps, could you fix them? If you can, we'd be very grateful."

"I could try. I'll have to ask my uncle."

"We'll pay you."

"Then I'm sure he'll say yes."

The officer said he would send a vehicle for Ari in the morning. Later, Ari told Jacob and watched as Jacob did a dance, he had wanted to sell the garrison something and Ari had opened the door. That night, Ari sat down and wrote a long letter to his parents. In the morning, he took it with him in the hope the garrison might have a post office.

Ari packed a few motors and water pumps in boxes and waited for his transport. Jacob was so excited he couldn't sit still. When a jeep arrived, they were both surprised that the driver was a sergeant major.

"Hello, I'm Bill from Coventry. I understand you are a Brummie lad? If you can fix my air cooler, I'll be eternally in your debt. The company that fits the coolers doesn't do repairs, crafty buggers. The army stationed in cold, old England doesn't understand the conditions here. Jump in, son. The sooner you fix things, the happier we'll be."

Ari put his boxes in the jeep, jumped in and waved goodbye to Jacob, who was in a trance.

"Have you seen much of Khartoum?"

"Very little. I've been stuck in the shop."

"We'll take the scenic drive along the Nile. There is no other scenery to speak of."

They soon reached the garrison and Bill saluted the Sudanese guards. There were two groups marching on the parade ground. It was getting hot and Ari was thinking — poor buggers.

"Our object here is to teach them to march and how to shoot their rifles. Teaching marching is difficult but many of them are good shots once they learn to use the rifle. I think most of them will make good soldiers and they'll be needed when war comes. And it will."

Bill was quick to show Ari the cooler in his office and Ari was quick to take it apart.

The cooler was full of sand, with the water pump partially blocked. The motor had been working under stress and had burnt out. Ari found the fan motor to be okay so he replaced the water pump, washed the straw and got the cooler going. After a spray of fine sand, the office started to cool. It was amazing how fast air coolers could work. Bill was over the moon and said it was cooling better than when it was new. Ari went around all the coolers and most just needed cleaning. The problem one was in the Sudanese soldier's quarters, where both motors had burnt out. A group of Sudanese soldiers watched in silence as he fixed their cooler, they had never seen a white man do this kind of work. When he switched on the cooler, they all stood up and clapped, Ari knew some Arabic now and they all laughed when he said that he needed water.

Bill took Ari to the Sergeant's Mess, where he was treated to water, then a cold beer. All the non-commissioned officers shook his hand and invited him to visit them any evening. Ari had forgotten how he had missed the company of English people. He was on his second beer when the captain walked in with an

Egyptian officer. The Egyptian was marvelling at how cool the room was and was saying he would talk to his commanding officer, as they had some poorly performing air coolers. The captain asked how they should pay Ari, it was decided on cash, as he did not know how Jacob handled finances. The captain would visit the shop the next day as he remembered he was after some cloth.

Ari left the mess and was greeted by Sudanese soldiers smiling and saluting him. The soldiers had loaded the jeep with lots of broken motors and water pumps. The drive back to the shop was full of stories about England. Uncle Jacob was so happy when Ari returned to tell him they would be paid the next day when the captain came for cloth. Jacob pulled out the best material he had and gave it a shake to remove the sand and dust.

The next day, the captain arrived with another officer who was introduced as the Military Attaché to the British Embassy. Jacob sat in the corner, mesmerised. The attaché wanted to know if Ari could look at some of the places the Embassy rented, as there were several broken air coolers. Ari said that he had no transport and if they could supply a car with a driver, he would be glad to have a look. Jacob couldn't believe it, here was Ari asking for an Embassy car with a driver. Jacob was also pleased with the payment from the army, although he tried not to show his delight. In the next few weeks, Ari earned more than the shop brought in and there was no end of broken motors.

One afternoon, a Rolls Royce pulled up outside the shop and a tall, very well-dressed Sudanese gentleman stepped out of the car. He entered the shop and asked for Ari. Abdul immediately recognised the man and whispered to Jacob that this was the richest man in Sudan, one of the Mahdi family. The man said he had several houses in Omdurman and asked if Ari would check out his air coolers. Ari again asked for transport and said he had not yet visited Omdurman. The man said that when he had finished the work, he would get a guided tour. The next morning, a Rolls Royce with a chauffeur in uniform came for Ari. The street was full of onlookers as Ari loaded his boxes into the boot. Jacob just watched in awe, Ari was king of Khartoum.

No one had realised the importance of the air cooler but in the oppressive heat of Khartoum, it was a must for work and for enjoyable living. The company importing the coolers realised they were losing business by not supplying parts so they started importing motors. Ari had the jump on them as he had many spares, the only spare in short supply was the carbon brushes for the electric motors. He found the Egyptian military could source them through Cairo, so he was laughing. Jacob decided that Ari should have a van and learn to drive. Abdul taught the young man how to drive and now Ari was very happy. He frequented the garrison where he picked up orders for things they stocked in the shop. The shop was getting a lot more customers because of Ari and Jacob was very pleased.

Abdul was going regularly to Port Sudan and picking up items that were unavailable in Khartoum. He was often reporting to Ari about the ships and the news from Europe. Ari was getting plenty of news about England but not so much about Europe and Egypt. He realised Abdul's news wasn't filtered, as it was from the British authorities.

Ari spent at least one evening a week in the Sergeant's Mess, where he would have a few drinks and hear news from England. He missed Ladywood but he had reconciled himself to staying in Khartoum. Bill told Ari, in July 1939, that he thought there would be a war and there was a possibility of conscription. He explained that all British males over the age of eighteen could be called up and that included Ari. Ari would be a problem as they would have to send him back to the UK for training and transport could be extremely difficult. Ari could be more useful to the British Army in Sudan, so they should prepare to try to get him an exemption.

Bill was correct, in September, war was declared and conscription came into effect. The Embassy and the army commander agreed that Ari was a difficult case and so he received his exemption. The next problem was Uncle Jacob, who was a German Jew. The British Embassy demanded that all Germans should surrender their passports but did not confine German nationals. Ari was telling his uncle to keep a low profile. Jacob understood, having seen the First World War.

Supplies started to dry up as the war progressed, the routes into Omdurman became more important. Ari's Mahdi connection was invaluable and Abdul was having a great time buying in the market and having tea in the big house. Ari was noting that his uncle was quite often unwell, so he took over running the shop and asked Jacob to rest.

It was during one of the days when he was in charge that two young girls entered the shop. They were both beautiful but the eldest took Ari's eye. He wasn't sure what they wanted to buy but was sure they were flirting with him. Jacob had heard the giggling girls and had peeped through the curtain. When they had left, he informed Ari that these were Jewish girls and their father was a doctor. In the next week, the girls came into the shop a couple of times and bought some small items. Ari was enjoying their visits and told Jacob that he was going to ask their father if he could take the eldest out. He had no idea where they would go but he had to try. Jacob did not look too enthusiastic but said nothing.

Ari found the address and late one afternoon went to see the father. He asked whether he could take the eldest daughter out (he cursed himself for not learning her name) and received a curt and sharp "**NO**" followed by "My daughters are banned from your shop." Ari was taken aback and did not know what to say so he retreated. Jacob was sympathetic but said that he expected a negative reply from the father. Ari decided to go to the mess and discuss it with Bill.

"Everywhere you go, there is some kind of class system. I assume this doctor thinks you are a class below him and his family. Just be patient. You'll find someone. I agree Khartoum is not the best place to look for a girl but one will come along."

Ari was quiet and consumed three beers rather than his usual two. Bill made sure he was okay before he left. There was little traffic on the road but there could be a stray goat or a drunken local. Ari remembered to find out the latest news on the war so he could tell Jacob.

Over the next few weeks, Abdul and Ari spent lots of time in Omdurman; Ari brushing up on his Arabic and Abdul on his English. The war was in full swing in the Mediterranean — more or less no trade was coming from Egypt or Ethiopia. The only goods were coming through Omdurman from across the Sahara or from the south, along the Nile.

Jacob had been looking after the shop but was a bit concerned for Ari. He had taken the rejection badly. Jacob had tuned into the Jewish chatter and learned why Ari was rejected and for better or worse, he had to tell what he had heard.

"Ari, I have heard why the doctor said no. He said you speak poor English, no Hebrew or Yiddish and you do not attend the synagogue. You have no need of

Hebrew and Yiddish, going to the synagogue is your choice and everyone understands your English. Forget that family — they are snobs."

"Thank you, Uncle. It's nice to know but it doesn't make me feel much better."

"Better you know the truth. Now, get on with your life."

Uncle Jacob was brutally honest and never tried to soften any blow but he was normally correct. Life in Khartoum for Ari was almost female-free and after a while, he carried on with his monogamous existence. Ari did not take his rejection well. He could have found a prostitute but when he thought about it, his parents came into his mind, why, he knew not.

Ladywood had taken a pounding from German bombers; the area was littered with industries. His father had sold the shop and moved to a better suburb called Quinton on the outskirts of Birmingham. His parents were both okay and enjoying semi-retirement. Ari knew his father could never fully retire.

The war was coming to a close but a new problem arose, Jacob was continually sick. Abdul and Ari took turns sitting with him, but he wouldn't see a doctor. Finally, Ari found an English doctor attached to the Embassy and invited him to see Jacob. He introduced the doctor as his friend and told Jacob he would be examined. This was the first time Ari had taken control. Jacob wouldn't take any drugs, nor have an X-ray. The doctor told Ari that Jacob had pneumonia and possibly a lung disease, but probably not tuberculosis. The lungs would have to be drained but Jacob wouldn't agree. The doctor had some diuretic pills but Jacob wouldn't even take them. Both Ari and Abdul tried to reason with Jacob but to no avail. There were days when Jacob would rally and then other days when he had trouble breathing. Jacob gave his will to Abdul and said to keep it for Ari, they were both taken care of in the will.

The war had ended and everyone was celebrating except for Abdul and Ari. Jacob was dying. Ari called on the rabbi and asked what he should do. The rabbi wasn't very helpful as he regarded Jacob as a lost soul. This made Ari mad but Abdul was a calming influence. He had learned much about the Hebrew religion and although he was a Muslim, he wanted Jacob to be buried in the Jewish way. Ari had learned a lot about religion in Sudan and marvelled at Abdul's sympathetic approach.

The funeral was conducted in the synagogue with Abdul standing outside. Ari understood very little of the ceremony but the little English that was spoken wasn't complimentary to Jacob. As they left the synagogue, Ari was in a foul mood, not improved when Abdul related what he had heard. A couple of men had said that Jacob wasn't a good Jew, they had said this in Yiddish but Abdul understood.

"If Jacob wasn't a good Jew, then I'm no Jew at all. I want nothing to do with these people, henceforth."

In his will, Jacob had left the shop to Ari, the lorry and all the cloth to Abdul. The rabbi came around for a donation and Ari told him to bugger off. Jacob had designed the business so that Abdul and Ari had to become partners, there was no problem as Abdul was indispensable and Ari was the future.

A couple of years passed and Ari decided they needed help in the shop. He wanted someone who spoke Arabic, English and possibly another language. He quietly looked around and found a young man who spoke the main languages, plus he understood Ethiopian. This young man, Sami, was an Iraqi Christian. Abdul approved so they hired him. His family had been in Sudan many years and his father was a doctor. Sami's English was passable, his Arabic was, of course, good and Ari liked his look.

Sami was smart. Liking to do things with his hands, he loved to take the motors apart. Ari had observed that many educated Sudanese were not keen on getting their hands dirty. Now Jacob was gone, Ari totally rearranged the shop, principally with Sami's help. Abdul rarely served in the shop, so it was of no importance to him.

One day, a beautiful girl came into the shop and spoke to Sami. Sami introduced Ari to Sara, she was his sister. She had black hair, dark eyes and white skin and the most appealing smile Ari had seen in years. Ari was so taken aback, all he could say was hello. That night, all he could think of was how useless he had been in front of the most gorgeous girl he had ever seen. Now he had a problem, she was Sami's sister, so what was his next move? In two days, Sara came into the shop when Sami was on an errand. Now Ari had his chance but he was lost for words. Luckily, Sara had the words. She had come for some cloth as her mother wanted to make a shawl. Abdul took over and gave Ari breathing space. He was enjoying watching Ari deal with a lady.

A couple of days later, Sami asked if Ari would like to come to a party for his dad's fiftieth birthday. Ari had been trying to figure out how to meet Sara and here was the perfect opportunity. Abdul could see the delight in Ari's eyes and was very pleased for his young partner. Ari had not been to many birthday parties since he was young, so he asked Bill what he could give a fifty-year-old man. He also confided in Bill that the most beautiful girl would be at the party. Bill suggested a bottle of very special whisky that he could let him have at a good price. Ari recognised that Bill was doing a good deal and he accepted and did not try to bargain. Actually, Bill gave him the bottle at the price he paid and Ari wanted to give him more. Bill was the best friend Ari had ever had except, maybe, for Abdul.

Ari arrived at the party and shook hands with Sami's father and handed over the bottle of scotch.

"How did you know I like scotch? And you have given me the best single malt that Scotland has to offer. This is a present I'll treasure."

Ari did not quite know what to say but Sami stepped in.

"My boss, Ari, has a way with people, he never shouts or screams and seems to pick a way to please everyone."

Sami's mother came and thanked Ari for making her husband so happy. Ari had worried that Bill's choice for a present might not be wise but now he thought him a genius. All the family was introduced to Ari and shaking hands with Sara was the highlight.

The food was plentiful and there was wine and some Ethiopian liquor. After the food, the dancing started. The men formed a circle and danced together; then the women formed a circle and danced together. Ari was wondering if men and women danced together at all, when the music changed and Sami's mother and father started to dance. This was the sign for other couples to dance. Sara came to Ari and asked him to dance. This was highly unusual and Ari admitted that he could not dance. Sara said she would show him but he wasn't to stand too close. This was heaven and hell, Ari wanted to be with Sara but on the dance floor, he was lost.

At the end of the dance, Sara went back to a group of giggling women and Sami came to Ari.

"I have never seen my sister do anything that extraordinary. It is so out of custom."

"She took me by surprise. I must learn to dance."

The party went on late into the night. Leaving at the end, Ari thanked Sami's mum and dad but couldn't see Sara to thank her. All night there was only one vision in his brain, it was Sara. The next day, he left Sami and Abdul in the shop, took himself off and sat by the Nile. He had never done that before but he had to get his thoughts in order. He then went to talk to Bill about the previous evening. Bill was very glad that the present had been a hit, he knew that many Sudanese drank and they prized the best liquor on offer.

Bill was both a friend and a father-figure and Ari spilled out his feelings. Bill's advice was to ask her father whether he could take Sara out. Ari remembered the last time he asked that question of a father. That situation was different, times were different and this father was a nice bloke.

Ari decided to throw caution and his fears to the wind and asked Sami's father the important question. Now he had to pluck up the courage and find a suitable time. Friday was a day when the shop was closed and Ari had plenty of time to sort out what he was going to say. The response was mostly positive.

"You cannot be alone, so her sisters or brother must be present at all times. You can hold hands but there must be a space between you. We would prefer you to be near our home and not be in a very public place."

Ari had licence but a very limited one and he couldn't say no to the conditions. Abdul laughed when he heard the conditions, they were very liberal. He had only met his wife once before they were married and going out together was out of the question. Bill also thought this was very liberal for Sudan. He listened to many of the Sudanese soldiers' stories and few would have such licence.

The first walk together was quite an event, the couple were in front, followed by at least twelve other people, mainly women. Ari did not say much but Sara told him her life story and a lot of her family story. She was taking the initiative and all he could see was her black hair, black eyes and smooth, white skin. He realised he couldn't kiss her, couldn't hold her in his arms. All he could do was look. In some ways, that was enough. He now appreciated that he had to do more talking when they next met. Ari realised he had not really taken a good look at her. She was wearing a colourful *tobe* (a stole made of fine material, used to cover the head, shoulders and arms) but he had not even seen her legs.

Ari started rehearsing what he would say on the next meeting but all he could think to speak about was Ladywood, that was it! He started to think that all he had really seen of her was her face. He had no idea about her body but the face was enough. He must take a better look next time.

The next meeting was dominated by life in England, particularly Ladywood. Sara's answer was that she would love to travel and Birmingham would be a good start. Ari's response to himself was that he had to marry this girl. She had listened to his disjointed talk and not said a word. Now he started to wonder what he had said.

After two more walks, Ari plucked up the courage to ask Sara's father whether they could marry. Sara's family were Catholic Christians, they must be married in the church, and any children would be brought up in the church. Ari wasn't religious but agreed to all those conditions. Sara had to agree to the marriage, which she did with great delight. Ari had to pay a dowry, in case the marriage did not work. He wanted to pay double the asking price but Abdul advised that the price was fair and Ari should cause no embarrassment.

Except for holding hands, Ari and Sara had never touched. He now started to doubt whether he was good enough for this beauty. As the day approached, he became more nervous. Bill was his rock, he kept telling Ari, that if she was the one he wanted, he must not hesitate.

The choice of best man was between Abdul and Bill but Abdul couldn't enter the church. So that just left Bill. Ari was quite apologetic but Abdul understood. Ari said that Abdul would be his best man outside the church and that news delighted Abdul.

The day came and Bill showed up at the church in full dress uniform, along with two of the other sergeants. There were a couple of people from the embassy and the church was full with Sara's relatives and friends. Abdul was waiting patiently outside the church with one or two of his relations. There was a Rolls Royce parked across the street with an interested fellow inside. Ari felt the service was too long but it would be all over soon, he hoped. Sara's veil seemed to be very thick and Ari could hardly see her face. Standing side by side, it was the first time he had noticed she was almost as tall as him. He thought she must have long legs and he couldn't wait to see them.

The service ended and Ari was thinking he could lift the veil and give Sara a kiss. She whispered that the kiss would be private, after they had signed the register. Although he was frustrated, he had to go along with the wishes of his new wife. The kiss was worth waiting for and he wanted it never to end. As they left the church, there was a cheering crowd but all Ari could think of was getting Sara alone. Abdul came and shook Ari's hand and bowed to Sara, there was a wave from the Rolls Royce and then the chauffeur saluted before driving away.

The reception was at Sara's home and one table was set out for the important guests. Sara's father gave a speech — half in English, half in Arabic — welcoming Ari to the family. Bill rose to give his speech and from his tunic produced a bottle of scotch and poured a glass for himself and one for Sara's father (he offered one to the mother but she declined). He then proposed a toast for the bride and groom and Sara's father was so pleased. Then Bill gave a short speech, again half in Arabic (he apologised in advance for the poor language) and half in English. The crowd started clapping and Sara's father came and shook Bill's hand.

Now it was Ari's turn, he gave his speech in Arabic. First, he thanked Abdul for teaching him well and then he marvelled at Bill being able to produce a bottle of whisky from his uniform. He then went on to thank Sara's parents for giving him the most beautiful wife in the world. That brought loud applause from the crowd. Bill was sitting with Sara's father and they both rose and raised their glasses. Sara's mother and sisters were crying in the background. Finally, Ari promised there would be a honeymoon later in the year and they would visit his parents in England. That also delighted the crowd. At the end of the speech, Sara nudged Ari and told him they now had to dance. Sara was taking the initiative.

The only good thing about the dance was that Ari could get close to Sara. All he wanted was to be alone with his wife. As they entered the floor, Ari realised all eyes were on them. Sara took control and guided him and to Ari's relief, Sara's mother and father joined the dance, followed by several other couples. After this dance, the men came to dance together and Bill joined the circle. It appeared that he had done this before and when the music stopped, all the men crowded around him, shaking his hand. Then it was the women's turn and Sara asked Ari if she could join the circle. Ari was used to telling people what to do or being told what to do but asking his permission was something new. He was flustered and finally muttered, "Yes, of course." He couldn't take his eyes off her, she was so graceful and obviously enjoying herself. Bill came over with a glass of whisky, which he offered to Ari.

"Your father-in-law is a doctor. We might be able to use him with our Sudanese troops. I'll talk to the commandant."

Ari was half listening but couldn't stop looking at Sara. As the dance ended, Bill was able to get his attention. "You have married the prettiest girl here. You're a very lucky Brummie."

"I thought I would never marry. In Khartoum there seemed to be little choice and now I've found gold. I can't wait to take her to England but she will find it so cold."

"Plan your honeymoon carefully, it has to be in the summer and the route could be difficult. There is a problem in Palestine and several British soldiers have been killed, that will have an effect in Egypt. Make sure you have passports, you have a lot of friends in the embassy so I would get new passports. I think, with what's going on in India and Palestine, the embassy here may get a shake-up."

This was January 1948 — probably the coolest month in Khartoum, but problems were heating up in the Middle East. Ari had a passport but had never thought that it was probably expired. All he could think about, at the moment, was to get Sara alone. He drank the whisky but realised he had to drive home with a precious cargo. There were lots of well-wishers. When they were about to leave, Sara took charge, telling them she wished to be alone with her husband. Those were Ari's sentiments but Sara had put them so well, she must be reading his mind.

Ari drove home and when they arrived, they kissed. It was quite late and no one was around. The bedroom was cool, Ari had put every effort into making the air cooler work at maximum efficiency. After a hug, Sara started to undress. Ari stood spellbound. She was nearly naked.

"Are you going to remain dressed?" she enquired.

"I apologise… I can't believe what I'm seeing. Please forgive me."

"You are only the second person to see me naked,' she said, ridding herself of the last garments. "Don't worry, the other person was my sister."

Ari was speechless. He had loved her facial beauty but now he saw her full body, he was seeing a goddess. She had long legs, small hips and small but well-rounded breasts and such lovely white skin. He now started to disrobe but couldn't avert his eyes. When he was fully naked, she came and gave him a long kiss. Her body was pressed to his and he became aroused. She pushed him on to the bed and mounted him. The sensation was incredible and Sara was doing all the work. She had taken control and he just sort of let it happen. As they lay together, he couldn't get his thoughts in order, he wanted that sensation again but if it did not happen, he would be disappointed. Sara took charge and said they should just hold each other close for a while. Sara must be reading his thoughts, all he wanted to do was hold her close.

The next morning, he awoke with Sara in his embrace. Her hair was a mess but that did not detract from her beautiful face. She looked so peaceful, he couldn't move. When she awoke, they lay in silence for a while.

"I should get up and make my husband's breakfast."

"Please, let's lie here for a while. I'm not hungry, except for you."

She laughed and they just lay still for about half an hour. Finally, she said "We must get up" and wanted to prepare his breakfast. Sara was taking charge again and he loved the feeling. She was a good cook, her mother had made sure all the sisters could cook. The next few days, Ari hardly entered the shop. He just wanted to be close to Sara. The shop was being adequately run by Abdul and Sami. Business had picked up after the wedding.

Sara entered the shop one morning, to say hello to her brother. After the normal greetings, Sami said, "Popa is so happy. He has a wonderful son-in-law and now a new friend. He was so impressed that they both gave speeches in Arabic and his family are telling him they had a wonderful time. He is going to the garrison to see if he can be of service with the Sudanese troops. The military doctor is on a tour of the garrisons and will not be back for weeks. I'm sure Popa will drink some whisky."

Sara laughed and asked how her mother was coping without her eldest daughter.

"Selina (the next eldest sister) has taken your place and now wants to find a husband. Moma is very pleased that Popa is happy, she thought he might miss you too much."

Abdul sat in the background, smiling. He had also enjoyed the wedding. Meanwhile, Ari was in the back of the store, planning his honeymoon. When Sara came back from the shop, he had to hug her. All the time he wanted to touch, hug or kiss her and now it occurred to him that she might feel overpowered by his attention. He decided to ask her.

"You are my husband. You can do whatever you wish with me."

"Now, I want to talk seriously to you. I need to get you a passport and to renew my passport. I plan to go to England in the summer, so you can meet my parents. At present, in January, it's too cold and also Bill tells me there is a problem in Jerusalem. The first thing is to get all your documents and the second thing is to plan our journey. First, I must ask you, do you want to go?"

"Yes — I have to go and would love to see England. I want to meet your parents to see if they approve of me. It's my duty."

Ari was thinking — how couldn't they approve of you. The next thing was to go to Sara's parents to sort out the documents. Sara's father was in a happy mood. Bill had introduced him to the Commandant, along with the Egyptian General in charge of their forces. He was now hired to treat any sick soldiers, whether Sudanese or Egyptian. While the military doctor was away, he could treat any British soldiers. The British Embassy had called to ask him to look after some of their junior staff. Ari had been the key to all this success.

Sara had a birth certificate signed by a registrar at the British Embassy. She had other documents, showing she had been a resident in Khartoum and a certificate from Unity Girls' High School, proving her proficiency in English and Arabic.

Popa sat down with Ari and thanked him for opening up a whole new world in Khartoum. All the family would benefit by knowing the people in power. Bill was now a friend he treasured, he never thought that military men could be so interesting and intelligent but he was learning new things. Sara's sisters now wanted to marry Englishmen but they were hard to find in Khartoum. Ari thought of his childhood friends in

Ladywood, they would fall over themselves trying to marry one of these beauties.

Ari started to realise he would need plenty of money for his proposed honeymoon, so he had better explore more ways to make it. Sami had learnt to repair motors and service air coolers; Abdul was still bringing saleable items from Omdurman, but Ari needed something new. He decided he would take his wife on a little trip, they would catch the train to Port Sudan. He wanted to talk to the import agent and some of the ships' captains. It was an overnight journey with no sleeping cabins but Sara did not complain, although Ari said he almost enjoyed the lorry trip more. Sara had never been out of Khartoum and it was many years since Ari had been to Port Sudan.

In Port Sudan, they lodged with the agent and Sara was fascinated by the sea but not by the humidity. Ari met several captains and they were all worried about the war in the north and the potential closure of the Suez Canal. Ari was looking for new products to sell in Khartoum. There was powdered milk in sealed cans, Khartoum had plenty of goats' milk but no cows' milk. There was tinned cheddar but in Khartoum there was goats' cheese; some in the form of fetta and some in a hard cheese, called twisted cheese. Tinned meat, especially corned beef, was coming from South America and that might sell well. From Kenya and South Africa, there was tinned fruit but there was plenty of fruit in

Khartoum, except for apples and pears. There was also drinking chocolate and that might appeal to the Sudanese.

Besides food stuffs, there were toolkits coming from Germany. This was good steel but was probably too expensive for Khartoum. Ari did not want to get into car parts and the importation of cars was out of his league. There was nothing he could find that would drastically improve his finances, so he ordered a few cases of this and that and would send Abdul to pick them up. He enjoyed a few days with Sara and took a boat out to the reef. This was the only time Sara was reluctant, she couldn't swim. Ari had not swum for many years. He had learned to swim at the baths on Monument Road. Sara was glad she came, as she couldn't believe the fish life she could see in the clear, blue water. Many times she told the story to her family and friends, of seeing so many fish she couldn't count them. Ari was pleased this trip had one success, at least.

The goods came to Khartoum and everything sold — even the expensive tool sets. The tinned cheddar and the corned beef rocketed off the shelf and the tinned milk and drinking chocolate were popular. Ari ordered more of these items and set about trying to decide what wasn't selling in the shop. He asked Abdul to go out to the camel camps to see if he could sell some of the unwanted items. He also put in some tins of milk powder and tinned fruit. Abdul came back having sold everything, the surprise was the milk powder. Once

Abdul had shown the Bedouins how to dissolve the powder in water, they were trying cows' milk for the first time. Normally, they lived on camels' milk. They pleaded with Abdul to bring all the tins available and they would pay with cash. When Abdul left, everyone — including women and children — were drinking glass after glass of milk and having a party.

Ari knew that the camel herders would spread the word and that tinned milk powder would be a big seller. Abdul was now making regular trips to Port Sudan. Sami asked if he might go on one of the trips, he was keen to see the sea. Sami was a good worker and it was a chance for Ari and Sara to be alone in the shop. He tried to spend as much time with Sara as he could, always trying to be close to her. Their love wasn't cooling, if anything, it was getting stronger. Sara had a way of directing Ari which he only noticed later. He wasn't upset but proud of his wife for taking the initiative. In family matters, Sara was in control. Even in dealing with some problem customers, she smoothed things over. Ari couldn't fault her approach to everything, nor did he want to.

Ari consulted the British Consul about their passports. His had expired and Sara did not have one. Using the details of Ari's old passport, a temporary version could be made available. Sara had a birth certificate signed by a registrar, she was born in the British Empire and now had a marriage certificate. She could also get a temporary passport that had to be registered in England. Ari had to fill out a new form for him and one for Sara. When it came to religion on Ari's form, he put NONE. He consulted the consul about changing his name, he wanted to be called Harry Gold, not Ari Goldheim. The consul advised that he could do that by deed poll in England but then a new passport had to be obtained. Ari could travel on his old passport and ask for the new passport to be sent in the diplomatic bag.

Ari's father-in-law was so proud that his daughter now had a British passport. Ari consulted Bill on the best way to get to England. The journey was a long way off but he wanted everything to be as smooth as possible. He wanted it to be perfect for Sara. She was still the first vision he saw in the morning and when she was present, he couldn't take his eyes off her. Bill advised taking the train to Wadi Halfa, avoiding the Suez Canal. From Wadi Halfa, they could take a boat on the Nile to Cairo, then take the train to Alexandria and catch a boat to England. Ari would automatically take Bill's advice but he had also thought that this presented the best route.

Bill had other news, he was being transferred to Aldershot. This was one of the biggest army camps in England and with his seniority he could well become drill sergeant major. Bill was loath to leave Sudan but this could be his last promotion. Ari was happy for his friend but really sad to see him leave. Ari's father-in-law was also sad to see Bill leave. They had become good friends.

Ari told Sara of the plans and she was excited. She wanted to see Egypt and to sail on a ship in the sea. At school she had enjoyed geography but now she was going to see the world for real. There was a big party for Bill and all the military brass were there, including the Egyptian General. Ari and his father-in-law attended and Popa was in awe of the ceremony and the respect given to Bill.

"He is no ordinary soldier. I can't believe his wealth of knowledge and his understanding of people."

"Yes, father. He has been like a father to me and his advice has always been correct."

At the end of the evening, they all shook hands and Ari hugged Bill. Bill sent his regards to Sara and warned Ari never to let her go and he expected to see her in England. Ari was never going to let her go.

Bill's expectations were not met. Within two weeks of landing in England, he was retired from the Army. He had a good pension but they had taken away his love. On learning of the retirement, the Egyptian General was irate, they would have hired him had they known in advance. Ari wanted to send for him to come to Sudan but his honeymoon was fast approaching.

The situation in Palestine was deteriorating and Ari was hoping it wouldn't affect his honeymoon. The shop was to be run jointly by Abdul and Sami while he was away. Sami had cajoled his father into letting Sami's sisters help in the shop, if needed. The sisters were overjoyed by the possibility of being able to work.

Khartoum to Birmingham

Ari had planned this trip and he had sent money to his account in Birmingham. He also opened an account in Egypt. He wanted to treat Sara to a special honeymoon. He also asked his Omdurman friend if he could use his car to take them to the railway station. Of course, the answer was yes.

The crowd at the station was large. There was even a troop of soldiers. One of the sergeants had marched them from the barracks. The soldiers appreciated Ari's work on their air coolers. After a hot day on the square, they could now cool off in their barracks. They also noted that their coolers were as good as those of the officers. Ari and Sara were quite overwhelmed by the reception but there was a slight delay so they could chat with several people. Ari was telling Abdul and Sami what to do, when Sara interrupted and told him to relax and that everything would be fine. Sara had conquered his nerves; something she would be able to do many times in the future.

The train to Wadi Halfa was without a sleeper but stopped at Atbara, where they could stretch their legs. The carriages were uncomfortable but Ari had not been north of Khartoum so he was interested in the scenery. Sara slept a while but did not complain about the uncomfortable seats. Ari just loved having her in his arms, although he often felt uncomfortable.

Wadi Halfa dock was quite small and there seemed to be a hundred people with all sorts of luggage. As first-class passengers, Ari and Sara were asked to board the boat first. Ari watched as the other passengers boarded and realised that most of the crowd were well-wishers or porters. That settled his nerves as he thought the boat would be overloaded. This boat was much more comfortable than the train; they had a small cabin with a bed. It was often cooler on deck but the privacy at night meant they were enjoying themselves. Ari went to the wheel house to talk to the captain, the Egyptian crew marvelled at Ari, who was speaking their kind of Arabic. He knew all the slang words and phrases and yet he could speak classical Arabic, they thought he must be a scholar. The captain informed Ari that they would have to change boats at the Low Dam. This was new to Ari. The captain assured him that all would go smoothly as the same company ran both boats.

Sara loved being on the water and she was determined to learn to swim. The scenery was magical and after boarding the new ship, they had a better cabin. The sight of Luxor had her shaking with excitement and her first sight of the pyramids was such a joy. She would have a lot to tell her sisters. All this and they were not even in Cairo. As they approached Cairo, she could see many more people and small sailboats. Everyone seemed happy, waving at them. There seemed to be cars everywhere and the smell of oil and particularly pungent petrol was in the air.

Cairo was so crowded. Ari had to do a lot of shopping for Sara. She needed sturdy leather boots and shoes, warm clothing and particularly, a warm coat. On his shopping spree he saw nylons, he had heard about them and seen them on a film in the sergeants' mess. He couldn't wait to see Sara in them and of course, he would have to help her put them on. The souk was crowded and Sara wasn't so keen on the hustle and bustle. Ari had warned her about pickpockets, bag-snatchers and bottom-pinchers.

"What are they?" she asked.

Ari took great delight in a demonstration. Sara couldn't believe that could happen in broad daylight but Ari said he would walk slightly behind her to protect her precious body part. Sara was glad to get out of the souk, unscathed. She was also relieved when they caught the train to Alexandria. Cairo wasn't for her.

This train was so full that people were hanging off the sides of the carriages. Luckily, Ari had booked first-class seats. The four-berth cabin had a wealthy Egyptian and a British civil servant going on leave. Ari thought he should address the Egyptian in classical Arabic and asked what he did for a living.

"I like your Arabic but doing something 'for a living' is a very English way of asking what business I carry out."

"I'm sorry — my husband mixed his English and Arabic."

Now the Egyptian sat back. "Are you both English?"

Sara said she would speak in English so as not to leave out their fellow traveller. "I'm Iraqi-Sudanese and my husband is English. We are from Khartoum."

"Now you have surprised me."

The Englishman now joined the conversation. "Are you going to England?"

"Yes. I have never been to England; my husband is taking me to Birmingham."

Ari was sitting back, letting his wife take over. He did not mind as he was thinking about how certain phrases translated from one language to another did not fit.

The Egyptian presented his card to Ari and said if they were in Cairo to contact him.

"I see you import cars. Is that why you are going to Alexandria?" Ari enquired.

"Yes, there is problem. The dockers are striking and refuse to unload my vehicles."

"That's interesting. Several years ago, on my way to Khartoum, there was a similar problem. I'm sure you'll sort it out but if you have to talk to the dockers yourself, you might use a bit of street talk. Sara — shut your ears."

Ari then told the man a few phrases and the Egyptian said, "You are truly amazing. I have not heard that language for years. I'll keep those phrases in mind but I'm not sure I could use them."

The Englishman turned to Sara and asked what Ari had said.

"Very bad street language with lots of bad words I could never repeat."

They all laughed and then Sara asked the Englishman where he was going in England.

"I live in Cornwall, at the very south of England."

The rest of the journey was filled with talk about England and Khartoum. Ari admitted that he had seen very little of England but he would see a lot more with Sara. The Egyptian had been to London and Coventry visiting car plants. The Englishman never said what he did in the embassy but admitted Cairo was an interesting posting. When they reached the Alexandria station, they all shook hands and went their separate ways.

In Cairo, the newly married couple had stayed in a small hotel, but Ari had booked a very upmarket venue in Alexandria. Sara was amazed by the staff, the porters, the housekeepers and the bar staff. Room service was something outside her imagination and the toilet with a bidet, bath and shower was a wonder. They were staying only a few days, while Ari found a suitable ship but she thought these the best days of her life. Ari was cautious on their trips outside the hotel but Sara just wanted to stay inside the hotel, where everyone was calling her madam.

Ari found a ship going to Southampton, they would have a cabin with portholes. The captain was English but most of the crew were Arab and Ari thought that might suit Sara. She was a little disappointed; she was starting to hear other languages and was enjoying the rhythm of speech. She was comparing Ari's English with the staff in the hotel, as well as comparing the Arabic of the boat crew with the Arabic of the hotel staff. One Italian had spoken to her in the hotel and his English was like a song. She told Ari about this and he thought she should hear a little of his dialect. They both laughed but Ari explained that she might have some difficulty with the way English was spoken in parts of England. Sara thought Arabic was spoken the same everywhere and English was English and it should be spoken the same everywhere. Ari did discuss with her the phrases in English that may not sound right in Arabic. After one session, with lots of laughter, they both enjoyed the afters.

When they arrived at the port, Ari was glad to see the dockers were not on strike. They boarded the ship and were greeted by the captain. The co-captain was Irish and Sara was enraptured by the sound of his voice. Most of the crew were from all around the Mediterranean and their Arabic was so different. She wrote a diary and it was full of the journey but also the people and their speech. She couldn't quite explain it but the sounds had become important to her.

Ari was hearing this from Sara and started to think how he could keep up with this whirlwind. This journey might give him time to catch up, because he felt a bit intimidated. Luckily, the sea took over. The Nile cruise had been smooth but the Med wasn't so calm. The first dinner at the captain's table had been wonderful but the next day the swell was rocking the boat from side to side. Sara could take it for a while but the constant motion was getting to her. Ari loved comforting her and suggested that being on deck, with a strong breeze, could be good. It was, but looking out to sea was no comfort. Ari suggested she shut her eyes and press her face to his chest. She admitted that the slow beat of his heart was comforting, while for Ari, the feel of her body close to him was enough.

They entered a few ports and the sounds of Italian and French were giving Sara so much joy. The really big surprise was Gibraltar. Ari had his arms around her as they entered Gibraltar harbour, her sea sickness had gone and she stared motionless at the sight.

"It is so big. Why is it so big? How can it be so big?"

"I can't answer those questions. All I can say is that I had the same reaction the first time I saw this mountain."

"My husband, you have given me a sight better than the pyramids. You are the best husband ever and I'm so lucky."

Again, they were not allowed to land.

"I'm going to come here one time and get into the city, even if I have to come through Spain," Ari declared.

Overnight in Gibraltar, Sara stayed up half the night looking at the lights. The captain apologised for not being able to land but the military were in charge and he could do nothing. The first mate was more succinct.

"They are scared some Spaniard could get on shore and spread propaganda, or an Irishman with a problem," he said, laughing. Sara was wondering what all that meant.

After leaving Gibraltar, the weather became cooler and Ari had great pleasure, in showing Sara how to put on nylons, and attach them to her suspender belt. Sara could have done it easily but she took pleasure in her husband enjoying himself. Sara now started to enjoy wearing her long overcoat. She had never worn any clothing so heavy. The swell was much bigger than they had previously experienced but Sara now had her sea legs and ignored the up and down and side-to-side motion. Ari seemed to be enjoying the motion a little less.

Approaching the English coast, the crew became excited, they were going to get shore leave. Ari was also full of anticipation, as he had not been in England for ten years. Sara was excited, she had enjoyed the ship but she would be glad to be on dry land. As they came into port, Ari hugged his wife. He was coming home. As they descended to the wharf, Sara said she felt wobbly and Ari put his arms around her and explained she had to get used to the ground not moving.

Ari had obtained a railway timetable through one of the sergeants and they could catch a train, mid-morning, to Snow Hill station. They had plenty of luggage so a taxi had to take them to the station. As they disembarked, the crew stood to attention and saluted. Ari said a few words in Arabic that made them all laugh. Sara wasn't quite up with the slang so she missed the punchline. The captain warned that Birmingham might be a culture shock and the first mate was telling her England could be a complete culture shock.

Sara was pleased with the train, the seats were so comfortable and clean and the carriages had been sprayed with a sweet-smelling perfume. When they arrived at Snow Hill, she was in awe of the station. It was so large, clean and organised. There were taxis waiting in an orderly line outside the station. They took a taxi to Quinton and on the way Sara asked, "What's that?"

"That's a double-decker bus. I'll take you on one tomorrow. We'll go back to the town centre."

"Yes, please."

Ari's parents knew they were coming but had no fixed date. Ari was hoping they were not out shopping but he was prepared to camp on the doorstep. In the event, Ari's parents were at home and the greetings went on for a good while. Ari's dad said that Sara was so beautiful, she could be a Jewish girl. Ari was quick to point out that she was a Christian and the best-looking girl in Khartoum. Ari's mother was much more diplomatic, saying that Ari had made a good choice and she welcomed her new daughter-in-law.

At dinner, Ari's father said a prayer in Hebrew and Sara said Amen. Ari was a bit on edge but Sara whispered that they must respect his parents. She was getting it so right but he could think only of Jacob. There was talk of the family, with most of them in the US — the ones that had escaped. The exception was Ari's mother's cousin, Simon, who was in Lagos. He had two shops, one being a tailor's shop. Simon was younger than Jacob but had gone to Nigeria before the war. Although they were from different families, Simon and Jacob were alike, they were adventurers. The news of relatives who had not escaped was grim, with none of them surviving the concentration camps. This was a sad moment for Ari and Sara. Ari's father had become more Jewish and religious. Ari wasn't interested in religion.

The next day, Ari and Sara took the bus to Birmingham. They entered at the back of the bus and climbed the stairs to the top deck. The top deck was for smokers but there were only a few on this bus. They moved to the front seat on the top deck. The conductor came to give them tickets. Sara asked what that was for. Ari explained it was the fare they had to pay for the ride and his young wife asked if she could keep the ticket. Ari was a bit amused but anything Sara requested he would automatically grant. Sara was looking everywhere; she was so excited, she kept nudging Ari to see some sight or other. When they alighted from the bus, in the city centre, she wanted to get straight back on. Ari said they should have morning tea in the Grand Hotel. He had always wanted to visit the Grand Hotel and now, with his beauty on his arm, he was going to enjoy the place.

The uniformed doorman ushered them into the lobby. It reminded Sara of the hotel in Alexandria but this one was more palatial. They were shown to a table in the restaurant. The waiter came to their table yet seemed a bit reluctant to serve them. Ari felt the waiter might be an Arab, so he asked. The waiter started to smile but when Ari addressed him in classical Arabic, he took two steps backwards and straightened up. Ari ordered tea and cakes and was amused by a little clump of waiters in one corner. The head waiter came over and asked where they were from and Ari told him Khartoum via Ladywood. Ari had fulfilled a dream to eat in the Grand Hotel.

Emerging from the hotel, Ari decided to find a bus stop. Sara was so keen to catch a bus that Ari decided that they would go to Five Ways and then walk along Monument Road into Ladywood. Sara was surprised that the queue was so orderly. The bus was full and they couldn't get a front seat on the upper deck but they did get a seat near the back. Sara was reluctant to get off at Five Ways. As they walked, Ari couldn't believe the devastation, there were so many bombed sites. At one stage, he wanted to turn back but he thought they must go on to the library. Sara was asking lots of questions but all Ari had in reply was "German bombers!" They reached the library and it was standing untouched. Entering, the librarian asked if she could be of help. Ari asked about an old soldier. The librarian did not know of such a person but she had been in charge only for a couple of years. As they left the library, Ari had a tear in his eye, this wasn't what he wanted to see. Sara sensed that he was sad and asked what he wanted to do.

"I want a pint, a baked potato or fish and chips."

"Where can we get them?"

"We'll catch a bus to the centre. I know you'll enjoy that. Then we'll find a good pub, there's plenty of choice. You've not been to a pub and you shouldn't do so without me. I'll find one with a lounge and hope they have scratchings."

"What are scratchings?"

"Roasted pig skin. It's a good job you're not a Muslim."

They found a good pub with potato chips and scratchings but fish and chips would have to be obtained elsewhere. Ari had his pint and Sara had an orange juice. After a couple of bites of scratchings, she left the rest to Ari. They took a double-decker bus back to Quinton and Sara loved every minute. Ari wasn't in such good spirits. Ladywood had been a disappointment.

The next day, they were off to London to get their passports registered. Ari had not told his parents of his name change. In fact, even Sara did not know what he planned to do. They would stay in London only a few days, so they needed just minimal luggage. Ari's mom had lent Sara a woollen cardigan and a pair of socks. Nylons did not keep feet warm. Ari would have taken a taxi but knowing his wife's enjoyment of the bus, he decided to travel that way. Having luggage meant that they had to sit downstairs but this was just as enjoyable for Sara, as she was fascinated by the conductor. This conductor was very talkative and it took Sara some time before she understood what he was saying. She had to ask Ari a few questions about phrases the conductor used. This put Ari in a better mood but he was now looking for bombed sites.

The train from Snow Hill was smooth, comfortable and on time. Sara had marvelled at how the countryside was so orderly and green. Her next surprise was the size of Paddington station. She looked up at the roof and couldn't believe how high and wide it was. There seemed to be many steam trains waiting to go and the noise was incredible. As Ari did not know the bus routes, he decided to take a taxi to the hotel. Sara's comment was that the buses were red and the taxis black.

They checked into the hotel and decided to find lunch in a pub. Sara wanted Ari to have his pint and she found pubs interesting. The pub had sandwiches and buns. Ari asked for two cobs but the quizzical look from the barman made him change that to buns. Sara enjoyed her cheese and tomato bun and decided on lemonade, which she also enjoyed. There were men at the bar speaking rather loudly.

"Are those men speaking English?" Sara whispered to Ari.

Ari laughed. "Yes — I think they're cockneys from the east of London, they have a different way of speaking. They have what we call rhyming slang, which I'll explain to you later."

Ari never did explain rhyming slang. In the afternoon, they took a red double-decker bus to the Tower of London. The queue to get into the Tower was too long but there was plenty of entertainment outside. There were jugglers and acrobats and singers. Sara enjoyed the entertainment. They walked to Tower Bridge and when Ari explained that the road opened up when a ship passed through, Sara just stared in amazement.

The evening meal in the hotel was typical English fare, roast beef and Yorkshire pudding. The austerity after the war had not yet relaxed and the menu was very limited.

"We must try fish and chips tomorrow," Ari declared. The double bed in their room was a bit soft but that did not spoil their enjoyment before sleep.

The next day was taken up with passports and the deed poll. Sara did not understand why they needed to go to several offices but she left it all to Ari. The registration of the passports wasn't simple, as new

83

passports were to be produced. Their photos from the old passports could be used and they had to come back in three working days. The deed poll and the production of another passport could take at least a week. Ari had planned for that, as it gave them time to visit Bill and go out into the countryside.

Back in Birmingham, Ari decided they must visit Bill in Coventry. Ari had an address but he had never been to Coventry. They set out early one morning and caught the train to Coventry and a taxi to Bill's place. Bill was so pleased to see them, he had a tear in his eye. He explained that when he arrived in Aldershot, he had no idea that they were going to retire him. When it happened, he was in shock and couldn't think straight for weeks. He realised he should have gone straight back to Sudan to find a job but he had lost all coherent thought. Now he had a few jobs in security but he couldn't settle down, so he was in semi-retirement. Sara couldn't believe how a trusted servant could be tossed out; she was definitely learning English phrases from Ari.

Bill said that there were a few old soldiers around and they would meet down at the pub but he longed for the Khartoum mess. The three of them went to the pub at lunchtime and met a couple of Bill's friends. They were impressed with Sara and Ari felt that all the pub patrons were staring at her. If she noticed, she ignored it. After the pub, they went to Coventry Cathedral, which was in complete ruins. Sara was so upset she started to cry. Ari had never seen her cry and all he could do was put his arm around her to provide some sort of comfort.

"Who could do this?"

"German bombers," was Bill's short reply.

Ari wasn't religious but he felt anger at the destruction. This was something he had to see, but in a way, he wished they were somewhere else. Sara was in a sort of shock, this was a cathedral and the Germans were Christians. How they could do such a thing? Bill took them to the station and wished them goodbye, saying he may never see them again. The train ride to Birmingham was completed in silence and Ari was glad to catch the bus to Quinton. At least it cheered Sara up.

The next day they took a bus to Warwick, it was a single-decker but Sara seemed to enjoy it just as much. Ari was thinking of the captain who had introduced him to a good living and Bill. They had a tour of the castle and Sara was very impressed. After lunch in a very old pub, they returned to his parents' house. Ari realised they were spending little time with his parents but he wanted to show Sara as much as he could. He found his father difficult, especially when the subject strayed to religion. Sara was telling Ari he should respect his father's views, a polite reminder.

Ari wasn't pleased with the city and decided they should get out into the countryside. One of the buses that used a bus stop close to the house went to Bewdley on the River Severn. They caught the bus but the front upper deck seat was occupied, so they decided to sit at the back. Everything was going smoothly until they reached a Y-junction called the Cross Keys. Ari noticed a lorry coming at speed on the side road. The bus was on the main road and the lorry was meant to stop — but it wasn't going to stop. Ari braced Sara and put one hand on the seat in front. The lorry hit the bus in the middle of the lower deck. Luckily, the bus did not roll over but landed in the car park of the Cross Keys pub, across the main road. Sara was shaken up and Ari was feeling his shoulder, but they were safe and thankful they were not injured. It was fortunate that there were few passengers on the lower deck and no one was severely injured, all the passengers climbed off the bus. Ari hugged Sara. This was the first time in England he had felt worried about his prized wife. Ari made sure Sara was okay and then started to talk to the army driver.

This army lorry had lost its brakes as it approached the intersection. The driver had frantically applied the handbrake, which had slowed the lorry but not prevented the crash. The driver was able to contact his base and someone there contacted the Midland Red Bus Company. A relief bus arrived within half an hour and the newly-weds were on their way. Ari was very relieved but Sara was amazed at how quickly the relief bus had appeared.

Arriving at Bewdley, it was a sunny day and they spent most of the time watching men fishing. After that scare, this was the most relaxing day they had spent in England. The town was small and explored in less than thirty minutes, so they then went back to a pub near the bridge to watch the fishing. On the way home on the bus, Ari sat very close to Sara with his arms around her.

The next day was spent at Ari's parents' house, relaxing. Sara helped Ari's mother with the lunch and evening meal. The ladies were getting on well. The following day, Ari took Sara to the city to see the Museum and Art Gallery and then to the Bullring to see Birmingham's 'souk'. Sara enjoyed wandering around the market and she bought a few trinkets for her sisters. Ari was entertained by the stallholders' banter and thought Khartoum souk could use a bit of spruiking.

The following day, they were off to London to collect their passports. Ari collected them and then went off to the Deed Poll Office. He collected the papers and thought it would be a mere formality to apply for a new passport. It wasn't that simple as he had recently (the same day) obtained a new passport. Ari argued that he had thought his temporary passport was just going to be registered and he had not requested a new passport. That argument fell on deaf ears and he was informed that his new application could take up to six months to process. After leaving the Khartoum Consul's name and address, Ari left the office in a bad mood. Sara had waited outside the office and did not understand what was going on. She sensed that something had gone awry but if Ari wasn't going to tell her, she wasn't going to ask.

Ari bought the Times newspaper to check on ship sailings, he wanted to go home to Khartoum. England had been a series of disappointments. Parts of Ladywood were bomb sites, no old friend in the library, Bill's situation and Coventry Cathedral and now this passport debacle had all made him reach a sudden decision. He told Sara that he had a feeling they must go home before the Suez Canal was shut. The canal was controlled by the British, who occupied the Canal Zone but if war broke out, they might be forced to shut the canal. The next day they went to Tilbury where Ari consulted several shipping agents. He found a ship leaving in about four days that would call at Port Sudan, if the canal wasn't closed. They checked out of the hotel and went back to Birmingham.

Ari's parents were disappointed but Ari explained he had to get back to Khartoum and if they could get to Port Sudan that would make the journey easier. Ari's father was proud of the state of Israel but Ari kept his opinions to himself, he felt there would be turmoil in the Arab world, and that included Sudan.

Birmingham to Khartoum

They spent two days in Birmingham and the farewell between the ladies was warm, demonstrated with hugs. The farewells with the father were less warm, with no kisses. The young couple spent the next two nights in Tilbury, as the ship was late. Both Ari and Sara spent time watching the ships and talking to sailors — they met several Egyptians and Iraqis. Ari felt this was the best time he had spent in England. Sara did not question her husband's hasty decision to leave but since coming to Tilbury, his mood had changed.

When the ship docked, Ari went to talk to the South African captain. The captain was keen to get through the Suez Canal and so far, the information was good. He had docked at Port Sudan several times and had cargo to offload. The captain explained that the crew were a mixed bunch with several Kenyans keen to go home. There was one Sudanese who was one of the stokers. Ari jokingly thought he might be able to stand the heat.

There was a cabin with two single beds which could be pushed together but there were very few facilities. Ari said they did not need entertaining and as long as he could hear the news and weather forecast, he would be happy. There were a few books for Sara to read but little else. Ari took Sara to a book store and allowed her to select several books, while he purchased some history books and maps.

The first mate was French. He had spent time in Algeria and knew some Arabic. Although the captain had said they might have no entertainment, it turned out to be an entertaining voyage. The Sudanese stoker was from the Nubian mountains and although he spoke Arabic, he had some words Ari had not heard before. Sara found out that he couldn't read or write, along with two of the Egyptian sailors, so she promised to help them. The first mate was also interested in learning how to read and write Arabic (he might have been attracted by the tutor).

Ari found that the Kenyans spoke Swahili, as well as their native language. Ari had heard of Swahili and knew it had Arabic words. They chatted to him in Swahili and they loved looking at his maps and were fascinated by English history. The captain was happy that half the crew were being entertained. Even the captain was interested in Khartoum — he knew of Gordon, the Mahdi and Kitchener but little else. Ari talked to the captain about his cargo and found much of it wasn't consigned and could be traded. He realised that there were several cargo items that could be sold in the Khartoum shop. He then started to bargain with the captain, as he had enough cash left, having cut short the trip. The captain was keen on cash, so they did a good deal.

As usual, they couldn't disembark at Gibraltar and Ari told Sara that, one day, they would land there. Ari was also keen to see Kenya and Tanganyika. Sara asked the captain if she could get more paper, as her Arabic script was getting through quite a lot of it. The captain was amused at the request but was able to get reams of paper from the local agent, who was also mystified.

Sara was fascinated with all the ports along the Spanish and French coasts. She couldn't get over the scenery. The captain told her they wouldn't enter any port in Italy but they would stop at Malta and then make straight for Alexandria. His ship was one of a dozen owned by the same shipping company and most of the Mediterranean ports were covered by other ships. His main object was to trade along the East African coast.

Docking in Alexandria the news was good, the Suez Canal was open. The dock area was crowded, as usual, and Sara marvelled at the porters carrying all sorts of cargo. She had not really noticed the activity when they last left Alexandria. The couple went to the market with the two Egyptians and the Sudanese. Every time they bought something, they would write down the item and the cost. The traders were bemused and couldn't understand what was going on. When they arrived back to the ship, the sailors were in fits of laughter. One of the Egyptians tried to explain some of the words the traders had used but Ari said he understood everything. The sailor was taken aback and tried a few slang phrases but Ari was able to answer back. Now, he had made friends for life.

The trip through the Suez Canal was uneventful, except there seemed to be lots of soldiers every mile. Sara couldn't believe seeing ships go through the desert. Some of the ships coming the opposite way were so large she had to crane her neck to look at them. She stayed on deck as long as she could and then went to the cabin to write her diary.

Ari was with the captain when they exited the canal, whereupon the captain gave a sigh of relief. He was South African, of Dutch stock, but did not regard himself as Afrikaans, the colour of sailors' skin did not matter as long as they could do their job. Ari learnt a lot about the system in South Africa and decided never to go there, but he would one day.

As they approached Port Sudan, Ari and Sara talked to the Sudanese sailor. They asked him whether he would leave the ship. His answer was no, he wanted to save enough money to go back to his village, build a house and buy a wife. He felt he did not quite have enough so, maybe on the return journey, he would leave the ship at Port Sudan. The Egyptian sailors more or less had the same idea. The Kenyan sailors were definitely leaving the ship at Mombasa. The captain knew of these events but he said there were many sailors at each port with tickets. The trick was to find good sailors.

They docked in Port Sudan and as they were leaving, the whole ship's crew came out to wish them goodbye. The captain and the first mate both said that this was the most entertaining voyage they had ever had. Sara had a tear in her eye and Ari was visibly moved, he was so glad to be in Sudan. They spent one night at the agent's house and then caught the train to Khartoum.

Back in Khartoum

Arriving back in Khartoum by train, Ari was so happy. He looked out through the carriage window and saw no changes. Ladywood had scared his memory. This was the height of summer but Ari did not mind. There had been no rain and so the humidity was low. The shop had not changed and Abdul and Sami were there to greet them. Ari was a bit reluctant but he told Abdul he had to go to Port Sudan to pick up some of the cargo he had bought. Abdul was delighted, he would rather be on the road than stuck in the shop. He was also happy to see them back in Khartoum. Sami was managing the air-cooler business although trade had slowed a little. He had identified a problem with poor wiring in many houses and was keen to become an electrician.

The couple went to greet Sara's family and found a big party. Sara was surrounded by brothers, sisters and cousins all wanting to know about England. Ari listened and all he could hear about was double-decker buses, climbing the stairs and getting a good seat. Ari's father-in-law asked about Bill. Ari explained that Bill was settled in a small house and had found some army friends. Ari was loath to share that Bill was very depressed and unhappy with the army. He described the bombing and his father-in-law was shocked. Very little information reached Sudan. Sara's mother had an interesting question for her new son-in-law, what had Sara learnt? Ari was taken a little aback. She had learnt to teach Arabs to read and write; she had discovered some English history; she now knew that England, even in the summer, was cold and that wearing socks and a cardigan was a must. Sara had seen more clouds in one day than she would see in many years in Khartoum and was surprised when there were days when the sun wasn't seen. She had learnt how to make fish and chips and Yorkshire pudding. Most of all, she had seen a different way of life. Ari wished that he could have put his words into some coherent order but his mother-in-law was satisfied. She was asking the correct questions.

"You have taken my daughter to another world, one where we could never have been able to send her. You have now presented us with a problem. How can we educate her brothers and sisters? We'll need your help."

Ari was now very emotional. "You are my family and I'll do my best to educate any of you as best I can."

Ari was on the spot, realising that he wanted all his relatives to have a good life. The girls were a problem, in this society, they were expected to get married and have children — not to work. That reminded him that he did not have children yet. In England he had seen many girls working in offices, generally using typewriters. In some of the hotels they were receptionists. He decided to buy a typewriter and went to the British Embassy. They had an old typewriter and as petty cash was low, they decided to sell it to Ari. Now the problem was to get it working. Sara took over and shortly she had it all worked out. It was in English typescript but that did not matter, she could teach her sisters and cousins to type and learn English at the same time. As most of them went to Unity High School, the use of English wasn't a problem. Ari's mother-in-law joined in the classes and every time she saw Ari, she thanked him. The next problem was to get an Arabic typewriter. The second-in-charge of the Egyptian garrison was still in Khartoum, although the general had been reassigned. Ari approached him and he was able to get a typewriter from Cairo (not cheap). Sara was enjoying herself so much, the price did not matter.

The boys were a different problem. One was able to go with Abdul to Port Sudan and stay with the agent to learn the ropes. There was some trade from the south, particularly Juba, but the journey was long and treacherous, setting up in Juba could be difficult. Abdul suggested one of his relatives wanted to go to the south, so two of them might be able to make a living in Juba. Ari consulted his father-in-law and they picked out a cousin who was adventurous.

The real problem Ari had was that Sara couldn't conceive. Ari consulted his father-in-law, who was also thinking about grandchildren. It was strange talking about sex with Popa, but he was a doctor. Sara and Ari had intercourse regularly so Popa asked for a sample of

Ari's sperm. A fresh sample was provided and when looking under the microscope, Popa said that the sperm count was a little low but not so low to present a problem. Popa then talked to Sara and examined her. He kept an eye on her through her menstrual cycle but could find nothing wrong. He could only advise they relax and not put too much thought into having a child.

Ari had more or less forgotten about his passport when the consul stopped by and gave him a new one, taking the old passport to be sent back to London. Ari made a big announcement to the family that, henceforth, he was Harry Gold. Some relatives wondered why anyone would change their name. He had told Sara first but she did not celebrate the change. He explained to her the whole process and why he was upset. Sara made a small complaint that he did not tell her when it was happening, but she said her husband must know best.

Harry was now very happy. He went to the British garrison and announced the change. They celebrated with a few beers.

Some years passed and in about 1955, his friend in Omdurman gave Harry a friendly warning. Independence was coming and British properties could be nationalised, including Harry's shop. Harry now decided he needed a change from Khartoum. Two of his sisters-in-law worked for embassies as typists, one for the British and one for the Egyptian. His brother-in-law in Port Sudan was now his agent and the one in Juba was doing very well. His father-in-law was a pillar of the community and his mother-in-law was doing well, keeping her husband's records.

He called Abdul, Sami and Sara together to discuss the problem. Sami was born in Sudan and could get citizenship. He asked Abdul if he would take Sami as a partner. Harry would sell his share for a nominal sum to make things legal. Harry had contacted his father. Their relative, called Simon, had a shop and a tailoring business in Lagos. Simon was getting old and had no children, he needed help. Would Sara be happy to go to Lagos? At least it would be warm there, unlike England.

"I'll go anywhere you want."

Lagos was also by the sea, with plenty of ships coming and going. Sara's response was that anywhere her husband went, she would follow. That short meeting settled everything. Now to tell the family.

Harry threw a party at his in-laws' house to celebrate his new name and to announce their future plans. When he announced that they were going to Lagos, the crowd went quiet. Harry thought that the family's geographical knowledge might be limited, so he had brought his book of maps and showed them Nigeria and Lagos. There was only one dissenting voice and that was Paul, Sara's youngest brother, who complained he was losing his teacher, Sara. Harry was touched by that comment, love for Sara wasn't his sole privilege. Harry also announced Abdul and Sami's partnership, to wild applause.

The speeches and toasts then started, and so did the dancing started. Harry and his father-in-law started to chat and they both agreed the family was doing well and was also prepared for independence. Sara was surrounded by sisters and female cousins all wanting to come to Nigeria (most of them also wanted to go to England). Sara warned that Lagos was hot and humid and England was so cold, even in the summer. She showed them her coat and they were all amazed at the weight. Her socks caused plenty of amusement. They all agreed that Harry was an exceptional husband but they couldn't understand why he would want to change his name.

In bed, that night, Sara wondered whether they were making the right move (this was the only negative comment she had made). Harry said he wasn't sure but they could come back to Sudan after Independence if Lagos did not work out. He thought that Independence could be good but there might be problems for the first few years. He was repeating the advice he was getting from Omdurman.

The next problem was how to get to Lagos. They could take a camel train to the north of Nigeria and proceed overland to Lagos. Harry discounted that route as being too arduous. The preferred route was to Port Sudan to catch a boat going south. Harry wanted to see Mombasa and practise some Swahili; Sara was also keen to see Kenya. From Mombasa, they would sail to Cape Town. The South African captain had described

Cape Town as one of the most beautiful cities in the world. Although Harry wasn't keen on the form of government, he was keen to visit Cape Town. Then they could catch a boat going up the west coast of Africa, a region totally unknown to Harry and Sara.

Sara was both happy and sad to leave Khartoum. She would never let Harry go on his own, she trusted him and always wanted to be by his side. The thought of all that sea travel excited her; she had enjoyed the ships and the ports they visited. She had one request and that was to go out to the reef off Port Sudan, the fish life was etched into her memory. Harry would do anything for Sara but this was an easy request he enjoyed.

In Port Sudan they stayed with Sara's brother, Ahmed. He was an agent for many traders and was very keen to impress Harry, which he did. The boat ride to the reef was perfect, the water was so still and Sara wondered at the vision. Harry was also pleased, there were far more fish than he had seen last time.

Port Sudan to Cape Town

Harry discussed the ships with the harbour master, who suggested one particular ship. This ship passed through Port Sudan regularly and was never a problem. The ship to Cape Town was captained by an Egyptian, who admitted that the Suez Canal was his countryman's route to captaining trading ships. Harry surprised the captain with his knowledge of Arabic, particularly the form spoken in Egypt. The crew was a very mixed bunch and Harry and Sara soon latched on to a couple of Kenyans. Harry spoke to them in Swahili and they just stood back, open-mouthed. Then he spoke to them in a pidgin-type English and they were still speechless. Sara piped up and told them not to be afraid. One sailor said that they were not afraid but astonished. Several of the crew had gathered around and they had varying forms of English but the best speaker was an Indian. This was going to be a good voyage.

Harry and Sara had plenty of time to talk to the crew as the captain had decided not to stop at Djibouti or Somaliland, so the first stop was to be Mombasa. The two Indian sailors were from Calcutta and they spoke very good English. They had left during the partition of India, there had been lots of killings in Calcutta and they felt they would be safer at sea. They had both been home and both had bought wives who still lived in Calcutta. Most of the money they earned was sent back to support their families, which included not only their wives but parents and siblings. One of the sailors voiced his thoughts quite succinctly.

"India was too big and all the politicians wanted power, so they carved it up, and in the process, killed millions of Indians. I hope one day we'll all be united and we'll have a big India."

After talking to this couple, Sara asked Harry whether this could happen in Sudan. Harry thought that some kind of separation could happen as Sudan was the biggest country in Africa. His friend in Omdurman had warned him that Independence might not be peaceful. In India, the major problem was religion — Hindu versus Muslim — but it could be a problem in Sudan with a Muslim north and a Christian and Animist south. Harry thought the Sudanese were a more peaceful people than the Indians, but he could be wrong.

Sara knew that they would be at sea for long periods so, unbeknown to Harry, she had sneaked a ream of paper into her luggage. She now started to teach sections of the crew to read and write in English or Arabic. Harry was interested in sailing and being able to understand charts. Dinner at the captain's table was very interesting. The conversation varied from language and geography to politics. The captain took Harry aside and said that Harry had married a most beautiful woman, who was intelligent and not intimidated by males. Harry agreed, everywhere she went she made a positive impression and she was his better at almost everything.

Almost all the crew were either studying with Sara or chatting with the couple. There seemed to be two exceptions, these sailors were from Persia. Firstly, they spoke Farsi and their English was poor. The second problem was they couldn't let a woman tell them what to do. Harry took them aside and with a bit of English and Arabic, he was able to find out their problem. He decided they should teach him Farsi by pointing at an object, giving the English name and asking the Farsi name. With the help of one of the Egyptian crew, he found they were Shia and then he started to understand the difference in the Muslim religion. The Egyptian was Sunni and the Persians Shia — a bit like Protestants and Catholics, only more confrontational. After a while, they could converse and Harry found they were both married with wives at home and that they also sent most of their wages home to keep the family. He tried to tell them they had a lot in common with the Indians but that wasn't understood.

When the captain announced they would dock at Mombasa, the whole crew became excited. They had been at sea a long time and only sighted land a couple of times. Although they were long-term sailors, they were a bit superstitious and had to see land occasionally.

They docked in Mombasa early in the morning and Harry noted a very strong smell of fish. There were several fishing vessels offloading their cargo next to their ship. The captain told Harry and Sara they wouldn't leave until the next day but to be back to the ship before dark. As they were about to disembark, the whole crew stood in a line to shake their hands. Harry explained in English, Arabic, Swahili and a crude Farsi that they would be back later in the day. The whole crew started clapping. All the crew, except for the Persians, shook Sara's hand but she understood their reluctance. The Kenyans were very effusive as they were leaving the ship. Neither of them was from Mombasa, so they would have a long journey to get back home.

It was hot and humid and Harry told Sara this was good practice for Lagos. What surprised Harry was the souk, which was full of all kinds of fruit and vegetables, many of which he had never seen and there was a variety of different smells. The other surprise was that all the shops were owned by Indians. He wanted a cold drink but was unsure of the hygiene, so he settled on tea. They sat for a while and drank their tea while watching the activity in the souk. Harry decided the only safe way to get a cold drink was to go to a good hotel.

A hotel close to the souk seemed to be suitable. They had fans, as air coolers would be useless in such a humid climate. The hotel was obviously run by Indians with Kenyans as porters and waiters. A waiter came to the table and Harry asked what cold drinks they had, first in Swahili and repeated in English. The waiter stood back.

"Your Swahili is very good but you have an interesting English accent."

Even Sara laughed and Harry said "You obviously don't get many Brummies."

"I'm sorry, sir, but what is a Brummie?"

Both Sara and Harry were laughing and the head waiter came over to ask if there was a problem. Harry said there was no problem but if this waiter worked for him, he would get a promotion. They had their cold drinks and decided that they would have lunch at that hotel. Exploring the centre of Mombasa was interesting, they could see the Arab and British influences in the buildings. The mixture of languages was fascinating both of them with their shared keen interest in language. Their walked along the road by the souk and entered a few shops. In these shops they were immediately confronted by Indian owners aggressively wanting to sell them anything. In one shop, Harry spied a small ebony carving of a Masai warrior, so he picked it up and weighed it in his hand. Khartoum was starting to get some carvings from the south but nothing of this quality. He showed it to Sara who frowned, she was playing the game (anything Harry liked she would automatically like). Harry started to put it down without asking the price and straightaway a price was suggested. Harry told Sara the price in Arabic and she shook her head. The price suddenly dropped by forty per cent and Harry started to speak in Swahili. The owner was confused. Harry thought it was a good price but he tried another tack. In his best British accent, he told the owner he would be mad to pay that price. The owner was almost begging them to take the figure and the price came down a little more. Harry finally smiled and paid the asking price. As they left the shop, he said to Sara that the bargaining could have gone on much longer but they had more to see.

Sara smiled. "That's a very good quality figure, the carving is superb."

Harry was wondering if he should let Sara do the bargaining for the next object.

As they walked, Harry was getting thirsty. In Khartoum, he drank water regularly but here he was sweating and drops were falling from his chin. He was now starting to wonder if Lagos was a good idea, he had never sweated this much in Port Sudan. He spied a building with a notice saying 'Members Only', so he caught Sara's hand and walked towards the building. It was a club. The receptionist advised them they could only enter if signed in by a member (even though they produced their British passports).

The only member in the club saw them at the reception and came over. "Can I help you?"

"Yes, we have arrived on a ship and would like to get a drink and relax for a while."

"Where are you from?"

"Khartoum."

"No, I meant in England."

Harry was tempted to say Brummagem but in his best English accent, he said, "Birmingham."

"I'm from Surrey. Where are you going?"

"Lagos."

"Khartoum to Lagos? That's one hell of a journey."

They were signed in and the man joined them at the table. Harry offered him a drink but he thanked them and said he had to get back to work, he was a bank manager.

After he had left, Sara said, "That man spoke in a very nice way. I liked his English."

"Yes, he spoke with what is called an Oxford or BBC accent."

They had their drinks and left, saying goodbye in Swahili to a surprised receptionist. They wandered back to the hotel and as it was nearly lunchtime, they sat and looked at the menu. Neither of them had had an Indian meal and the menu was full of curries.

"What's a samosa and how hot are the curries?" Harry asked.

"A samosa is a triangle of pastry with spicy meat inside and curries can be of varying strength. If you are not used to curry, I suggest the korma. It's our mildest curry."

They ordered the samosas and a korma goat curry. The samosas were delicious and Harry ordered more. The curry was also very good and they sat for a while to digest the feast. Leaving the hotel, Harry suggested they go back to the ship, as he wanted a rest. Sara also wanted a rest. On the way back to the ship, they met the cook with two Kenyans, carrying heavy bags. Harry greeted him and asked if he could cook samosas. The reply was now that he had fresh meat and vegetables, he could cook anything. During the voyage from Port Sudan, the only meat was tinned corned beef, the rest of the supplies had been dried beans, lentils, chick peas and rice. Now the next stop was Zanzibar, where they could buy fresh vegetables, and then Dar Es Salaam, where they could buy fresh meat. The cook said that as the meat could be tough, he minced it. That was just right for samosas and they would have them tonight.

Harry and Sara lay down for a short nap, which turned out to be two hours. Being near the equator, it would be dark at about five thirty, so they decided to explore only the port. There were several ships docked, including a Royal Navy destroyer. There was a group of armed sailors guarding the ship and Harry entered into a discussion with some of them. They were from all parts of England but none from Birmingham. They were on guard as the Mau Mau were still active and might want revenge for some recent executions. Harry had not thought about security with his most precious beauty by his side. He thought they should go back to the ship.

The evening meal was a treat; the food was the best they had eaten. The cook was giving them a feast. At the table, the discussion came around to food. The captain was talking about problems on a ship.

"Illness is always a problem when you are far from port, sometimes you cannot avoid crew being sick but food poisoning is avoidable. When the cook brings fresh meat, I make him cook it all and what is not consumed in three days is tossed overboard. Although we have a cold room, fresh meat cannot be stored and cooked meat cannot be stored for more than a few days. Tinned corned beef is our saviour."

Harry noticed they did not have fish.

"Although I live on the sea, I'm very wary of sea food. I let the crew try to catch fish off the stern of the boat and if they catch anything, they eat it that day. I like sea food but I'll only eat it in the best restaurants."

Sara asked why there were not more pastries.

"We can't store flour, it always gets insects, so if the flour is not consumed in a few days, I make the cook bake hard biscuits, the break-your-teeth type."

At the end of the dinner, the captain enquired of the crew if any crew member was missing. Apparently, two were missing. The two Kenyans who were on the ship from Port Sudan had resigned and two new crew, also Kenyans, had been hired. The two missing crew were Egyptians. Later that night they showed up, with one supporting the other. One was so drunk he could hardly stand. The captain asked what had happened. The more sober sailor said that he had just drunk beer but his friend had tried palm wine. The captain was angry but he told Harry that there could have been anything in that wine, but he hoped the sailor would be okay. If he were unwell the next day, he would have to be left in Mombasa. Sara thought that a bit drastic so she started to nurse the sailor.

She found a pillow for his head and forced him to drink lots of water, much of it coming straight back. Harry was watching.

"This is a self-inflicted problem," he said.

"One small mistake getting drunk is not the same as a big mistake, leaving him in Mombasa."

Harry had just had a polite rebuke — a first. He moved off to sit with the captain who said, "You have a character for a wife." Harry knew Sara had a strong character and it made him love her even more.

In the morning, they found the drunken seaman swabbing the deck where he had been lying, despite his tremendous hangover. Sara went to him and shook his hand, relieved that he wouldn't be left in Mombasa. On a long voyage the crew tends to unite and this crew were united, especially in praise of Sara. Even the two new Kenyan crew members were amazed at a passenger helping a crewman. Each crewman said "Thank you, madam," whenever they saw her. Harry had a chat with the new crew; it was more like a one-way conversation. The sailors just stood silent and open-mouthed as, in Swahili, he welcomed them to the ship.

As they were leaving Mombasa harbour, one or two of the crew caught fish. The fish were cooked and before anyone ate, a portion was offered to Sara. Harry stood back and clapped as she ate a small portion. He was looking forward to his samosas but he tried some fish. He had not eaten fresh fish for many years, except for fish and chips in England.

The captain explained that they would berth at Zanzibar, where he had a large consignment of goods and hoped to pick up yet more. Zanzibar was a trading island and a profitable place to do business. Arabic was the language used on the island, although their Arabic was a little bit different. Harry and Sara were excited to hear this version. As they docked, they could see the Arab influence in the clothing the men were wearing; also, there were almost no women in sight. As they walked through the market, they were each listening to the sounds and drawing in the smells. The smells were also different, this island smelled of spices; some sweet, but most, quite pungent. There was also the smell of cooked meat or fish. As they walked to a hotel, they noticed there were only men; no women.

They entered the hotel, where the receptionist spoke in very good English, directing them to the restaurant. As there were few people there, the head waiter came over. Harry decided to try his best classical Arabic. The waiter stood back and smiled.

"Your Arabic is very good and in the Middle East you would have been totally understood. Our Arabic has lots of older words from seafarers and also, we have incorporated some local language words, but not quite Swahili. Shall we try in English?"

Harry and Sara were delighted and in English, Sara said, with a smile, "I could try Iraqi Arabic."

Now all three were laughing. The waiter was summoned, the order taken and the head waiter sat down at the table.

"Where are you from?"

"Khartoum."

"I can't remember having a visitor from Khartoum. Before the war we had many European visitors, mainly English, German and French, but during the war almost none. The number of visitors is picking up but business is still slow. By the way, when your lady mentioned Iraqi Arabic, I had shivers down my spine. I was born in Damascus and have visited Baghdad many times but not for many years. I loved Baghdad and now I just assumed you were English scholars."

Harry was so proud to be called an English scholar and Sara was proud to be thought of as English. She admitted that she had never been to Baghdad but would love to go one day. She told him her family had left Iraq many years prior to her birth.

"Where are you going?"

"Lagos."

"This coincidence is incredible. I have a younger brother in Lagos. Khartoum to Lagos is quite a journey. Are you doing it all by ship?"

"Yes, we caught this ship in Port Sudan and will leave it in Cape Town. Then we'll catch another ship going along the African west coast."

"Such an interesting journey. You'll have been along almost sixty per cent of the African coastline. I'll write my brother's name and address in Lagos and the drinks are on the hotel."

Sara and Harry had both enjoyed the conversation and they set out to see the architecture. This was the most Arab city they had seen, the buildings were mainly old but even the new ones seemed to fit into the style. The carved doors were something to behold and some were so large that Harry wondered where they obtained the wood. Sara had a few stares in the market but when she started to speak Arabic, the stares became polite smiles. Not many of the stallholders would speak directly to Sara, they directed their conversation to Harry. Sara did buy a few trinkets in the market but Harry was a little put out that they wouldn't speak directly to his wife. They both agreed this was a fascinating island.

Back onboard ship, they related their adventures to the captain. He wasn't surprised as this was a very conservative society. Men would generally only speak to their mothers, sisters or wives. Times were changing but Zanzibar's isolation slowed down the change. The captain loved to come to the island as the bargaining was fierce but everything was settled on a handshake.

That night, the ship started to rock more than normal. In the morning there was a gale blowing. The captain explained that in these latitudes, gales can sometimes strike up off the Indian Ocean. This gale wasn't going to stop them travelling to Dar Es Salaam, but it could be a bit rough. It was rough and both Harry and Sara came close to sea sickness. There was relief as they approached the Tanganyika coast, where the gale subsided and they sailed into Dar Es Salaam harbour with almost no wind at all. This was a bay with lots of sailing boats and dhows and there were many sailors greeting them. The captain explained that sailing was popular in this area. The only problem was when a good gale approached, most of the yachts had to seek refuge. There were plenty of fish in this area and fishing was very popular.

Dar Es Salaam was like a smaller version of Mombasa. The market was similar but far less crowded. The shops were owned by Indians and some of the buildings had a European look, but not identifiable as German, Tanganyika had been a German Colony. The Swahili was slightly different due to a local tribal influence. Harry tried his Swahili in the market and there were plenty of smiles. One trader identified his version as Kenyan and corrected a few words into the local version. Sara received a better reception in the market than she had in Zanzibar; some of the stall holders had a long conversation with her. She commented that the smell of the market was like musty cloves mixed with wood smoke. Harry agreed that every port had a unique smell and sound.

The captain was happy as they sailed out next morning. The agent had secured lots of goods saleable in South Africa, including animal skins. Harry and Sara saw an abundance of fish life and some of the sailors caught quite sizable specimens. Sara was delighted by the flying fish that seemed to be following the ship.

Next stop, Lourenço Marques. This Portuguese city was always good for trade and they had an efficient port. The captain explained that everything was run by Portuguese and the only natives would be porters on the dock. Their passports should let them in for a day without a visa but he had never had British passport-holders landing at this port. He warned they should be very patient with the local authorities.

'Everything will be in Portuguese and I think you might have problems. I'm told you should try the prawns. But only in a hotel."

As they sailed into Lourenço Marques, the port looked so orderly and tidy. There were big cranes and several ships in the dock. The ship was guided into port by a Portuguese pilot, with two tugs alongside. Harry was on the bridge enjoying the spectacle. The captain was standing back, allowing the pilot to give all the orders. As they docked, Sara was standing near the captain and the crew were all standing in a line on the rails.

"This looks a very orderly dock. Will any of the crew be able to go into the city?"

"No, madam. Even I won't be able to leave the dock. I'll have to see the harbour master and our agent but only you and your husband will be able to go ashore, I think."

"Well, captain — this could be a different experience."

"I'll be very interested in your thoughts when you get back."

Harry and Sara disembarked with the captain and they made their way to the Customs and Immigration. An officer stopped them and motioned for their passports. He said something in Portuguese, which neither Harry nor Sara understood. A senior officer was called over. This officer explained that they did not get many British and asked how long they were staying. His English wasn't too good but they understood what he was asking. Harry explained they were only in the city for the day and wanted to see the sights. The officer gave a flick of his hand, indicating the customs man should go elsewhere. Harry looked at this gesture but said nothing. The officer said they could go but to be back before dusk. He also warned not to go outside the city centre.

Harry and Sara were silent as they left the port but as they walked towards the centre of the city, they could only see Portuguese, no Africans. There were some beautiful buildings, particularly the old houses. Harry remarked that at the Khartoum mess he had seen cowboy films with similar houses, he thought they were called *haciendas*. As they walked, they saw Portuguese walking, on bicycles, on motorbikes and in cars, but not one African. It was hot but the humidity was much lower than Dar Es Salaam. Harry told Sara he found this place weird.

They saw a ruined fort; the town hall was very impressive but none of the buildings had any African influence.

"I see no black people," Sara remarked. "Even in Birmingham, I saw a few."

"Yes, I was thinking the same myself," Harry agreed. "I find this town interesting but I'm uncomfortable. Everywhere we have been, there has been some kind of mix of people and sometimes I'm the only white man, but this is different."

They decided to have an early lunch and relax to assess the situation. Harry had money, dollars, pounds, Egyptian pounds and Kenyan shillings but of course, no local currency. Having a meal in a hotel could be interesting as they spoke no Portuguese. The male receptionist spoke a little English and directed them to the restaurant. They sat and a Portuguese waiter came over. Harry tried English, Arabic and then Swahili. The waiter stood and frowned, so the head waiter came to their table and waved the waiter away. At least this man had some English. Harry asked for cold drinks. At least the waiter understood beer and water (for Sara). Then Harry wanted prawns and now they couldn't communicate. Luckily, a man at another table spoke English and came over to help. He was South African and was living in Lourenço Marques. He ordered the prawns, which were very delicious, and asked where they were from and where they were going.

"Khartoum to Lagos," Harry responded.

"That's a new one on me. We get a few travellers to this city but you must be the first on such a journey. I have lived here ten years and I see many ships come to this port, as I'm a trader, but you have surprised me. What do you make of this city?"

Harry was glad someone spoke English. "I want to ask a question, but first — are you Afrikaans?"

"No, my family is of English and French stock."

"Entering this city, we have seen no black Africans, everything is Portuguese. All the staff in this hotel and everyone on the street seems to be Portuguese. Why?"

"There are Africans but they are not allowed into the city centre. Many of them work as servants in the big houses but if they leave, they must go outside the central city. Even most manual jobs are carried out by Portuguese."

Sara intervened. "You mean, there is no local market where the natives sell their produce?"

"No. Many of the Portuguese send their servants to the market outside the city but they would never go themselves. They love fish but there are no Portuguese in the fish market."

"This is not a place for me," said Sara. "I have even noticed a class system within the Portuguese. The way the immigration officer flicked his hand, telling his junior to go away, made my stomach tense up."

"Yes, there is a class system here and in many ways it's worse than in South Africa. All the Portuguese have a station and it is hard to get out of that station. My office manager is sort of classed as middle rank, but he bows when someone of a superior rank enters the room."

As they walked back to the ship, they both agreed it was an interesting place but they had seen enough. They were glad to be getting back to the ship. This was the first disembarkation where their language skills had been no good. Back on board, the captain was smiling at their experience but he was glad they enjoyed the prawns.

"Durban, next stop. You'll see a new country."

"We look forward to seeing this new country. Sara wants to buy a shawl, why, I'm not sure."

Sara smiled and asked the captain what Lagos would be like.

"I have never been to Lagos, so I can't tell you. From what I hear, it can be a rough place. Many ships pass through the Lagos Port and most of them meet in Cape Town. There is a set of ships, like mine, that do the east coast and others that do only the west coast, we meet in Cape Town and tell tales. Most of the tales I hear from Lagos is that it is a very vibrant city with lots of nightlife but a fair amount of crime. The sailors are warned about the liquor and the prostitutes, both can be strong and ruthless."

As they sailed into Durban, the crew were looking forward to leave, apart from the Kenyans, they would stay on board. Sara asked them why no leave and the basic answer was that there were too many restrictions and they would often have to identify themselves. Even the Egyptians said there were many restrictions, but it helped to have a well-known captain.

The port was as well organised as in Lourenço Marques and there were many cranes and ships in dock. The captain explained that there was a large manufacturing area nearby and many of the exports and imports involved metal objects, as well as tinned fruit.

"I sold a lot of those tins in Khartoum and some of the best customers were the Bedouin. I think most tins came from Kenya."

"I must remember that when I travel back to Port Sudan. You have given me lots of information on this trip."

Customs and Immigration took a cursory look at their passports and did not even ask how long they were staying. The dock area was very large and bordered by an industrial estate. They walked for a while and saw a policeman, so Harry decided to ask whether the town centre was close. This black policeman advised taking a taxi as it was too far to walk. First, they had to find a bank and the policeman pointed towards the end of the dock. This little bank was accustomed to changing foreign money but declined changing Sudanese pounds.

As they left the bank, Harry and Sara had a good laugh at Sudanese pounds not being recognised, being worth more than the pound sterling.

Sara asked Harry about the policeman.

"He had fairly good English," replied Harry, "but his accent was very strong. It took me a while to understand what he was saying. I assume my wife understood everything."

"You are the expert — I leave it to you."

"Your husband understood almost everything as the policemen's accent was a little different to the Kenyans. He told us what we wanted to know and it was important to know the location of the bank. We needed to change money as we'll visit Port Elizabeth and stay in Cape Town a few days."

"I'm glad you're in control," Sara said, with a smile.

After changing some money, they caught a taxi to the centre of town. The first thing they noticed was that there were black and white people on the street. The next thing they noticed were signs saying 'Whites Only', the first one on a water fountain. There was also a sign saying 'Coloureds Allowed'. They both recoiled at these signs and almost took a taxi back to the ship. All the hotels had repugnant signs, so they entered one with the sign 'Coloureds Allowed'. Even then, when they sat down in the restaurant, they found the seating was segregated. They ordered a snack and decided to go back to the ship, they were both in a poor mood. Harry admitted the beer was good.

Back onboard ship, they sat for a while on the deck without speaking. Finally, Sara took the initiative.

"Sami had told me so much about you, I had to take a look, that's why I came to the shop the first time. I liked what I saw and came to the shop the second time, when I knew Sami would be absent. I talked my father into inviting you to his birthday party and when I went against custom and asked you to dance, that was it."

"You snagged me from the first time I saw you, but why the confession now?"

"I saw your disgust at those signs. And Sami had told me you treated everyone equally and that attracted me to you. He also told me you were handsome and that I had to see for myself. I was getting old for an unmarried woman and I had a couple of suiters who were hopeless, so I had to take the initiative."

"I love the way you often take the initiative. From the first moment I saw you, I was captured, you just had me."

"Sami also told me he had never heard you raise your voice to shout. I hate people shouting; in some markets, the human noise is too much, it makes me nervous."

"Now I know I was a target and you hit the target but I hit the bull's eye."

"Today you lived up to my expectations. I could see you were angry at those signs but you kept your anger inside. I was very happy when we returned to the ship."

They retired early to a very enjoyable evening. At dinner, the captain was agitated and Harry asked what was wrong.

"I just had to get one of my men released from the police cells. He couldn't produce his ticket. He swears he had it on him when he left the ship. Probably some pickpocket has it, wondering how he can make money with the document. My countrymen are treated as coloured and have to produce identification. Luckily, his companion contacted me. Durban is a rough place and I'm tempted to ban shore leave when we return here. I telegraphed our agent in Cape Town to get the man another ticket but if one can't be obtained, he stays on the ship till we get back to Egypt. Port Elizabeth is similar to Durban but Cape Town is more relaxed, they're used to more foreigners. Here, the apartheid system is strong and I'm afraid the whole country will become like this, so we have to enjoy Cape Town while we can."

After the experience in Durban, Harry and Sara had determined not to disembark at Port Elizabeth. They both agreed that Durban was a real disappointment; in some ways more than Lourenço Marques. The whole crew decided not to go ashore in Port Elizabeth. They realised any one of them could lose their ticket. Harry talked to the Kenyans and asked if they would go ashore in Cape Town. They had both been in Cape Town before and knew places to go and areas not to go. They always carried two pieces of identification.

Harry asked the captain the quickest way to get a ship to Lagos. The captain contacted the agent, who sent back a list of ships and approximate sailing dates. Harry had decided to spend as little time in Cape Town as possible. The captain explained that Cape Town was a city with many nationalities and the apartheid control wasn't yet in full force. It had some good hotels and a couple of restaurants where even he would eat the sea food. He advised they find a hotel away from the dock area, as that location could be a little rough at times.

As they came into Cape Town harbour, both Harry and Sara stood on the deck amazed at the sight. First, there was Table Mountain towering over everything. Second was the number of ships (of all sizes) in the harbour and third, the buildings on the shore line. The architecture had an obvious Dutch influence but there were some odd shapes.

"This mountain is different to Gibraltar, this one has a flat top. Do all big harbours have big mountains?"

"I'm not sure. We'll have to check that out on our future ride up the west coast."

When Harry and Sara were leaving the ship, the whole crew lined up and saluted them. One of the Kenyans was almost in tears. He said that, one day, he would come to Lagos to visit them. The captain had the same sentiments and said he might try to get a ship on the western coast. The east coast had become boring and he would like to visit new places. These were the best passengers he had ever had the pleasure to entertain and they were going to see ports he had never visited.

Harry and Sara took a taxi and asked to go to a family hotel near but outside the dock area. The taxi driver turned out to be Lebanese and once Harry realised, the conversation flowed freely. The driver was so emotional when Harry talked to him in Arabic. When Sara chimed in, he stopped the car until he composed himself and then drove on.

"I've been in Cape Town many years with many passengers but you have both spoken my language so perfectly. Where are you from?"

"We are from Khartoum in the Sudan, where they speak the best Arabic."

"I want to argue with you on that point but your Arabic is so good, I might lose the argument. I'll go home tonight and tell my wife that I need to learn more Arabic. I'll take you to a very good family hotel and I hope you speak Italian."

Harry and Sara thanked the driver and booked into the hotel run by Italians who seemed to speak English with a strong Dutch accent. The owner admitted that he was born in Cape Town but his parents were Italian. Sara's comment to Harry was that he spoke nothing like an Italian. Harry left Sara to unpack a few clothes as he said they would be leaving in two days. Harry was a bit optimistic as the earliest they could leave was, in fact, four days. That evening they had a very good pasta meal and the owner came and sat at their table.

"Where are you going and where have you come from?"

"We came from Khartoum and we're going to Lagos by sea, via the Indian and Atlantic oceans."

"I know where Lagos is but where is Khartoum?"

Harry and Sara both smiled to each other. Now for the geography lesson. Harry drew a rough map of Africa on a napkin and drew Sudan, Khartoum, then Cape Town. Harry also drew Egypt and Cairo. The owner became excited and said his chef was from Egypt. Harry told him to call the chef. The chef came out, expecting a problem but when Harry spoke to him in Arabic, he almost started to cry. They hugged and the chef said he had not heard 'his' Arabic for many years. Sara thanked him for a fantastic meal and he was now in tears, bowing continually. The owner was amused but he had to send his chef back to the kitchen.

This hotel was clean, well run and friendly and Harry was thinking they should stay longer. Around the hotel there were many small shops and only one was run by Indians. Harry was interested in what they were selling and Sara was interested in the garments. Sara was very happy with Cape Town but she always wanted to go back to the hotel for the evening meal. The chef found okra but couldn't get molokhia; the owner thought that okra wasn't a vegetable he might use but was happy that Harry and Sara enjoyed their dish. The chef was so happy he kept coming from the kitchen to check everything was okay.

Harry was often at the dock, negotiating the passage and also looking at the cargos. He was interested in the ships going to Lagos and what they were carrying. Sara was just enjoying listening to the multitude of languages and accents. She determined she must learn another language but she couldn't decide on which one would be most useful. She later learnt that it wasn't a European language.

On their last night they both agreed that Cape Town wasn't so bad and they had picked the best hotel. They were now out to sea again, happy but also a little sad. The Italian owner was telling them to come back soon and the chef was saying he would try to get to Lagos.

Cape Town to Lagos

The new ship was bigger than the one from Port Sudan and was captained by an Englishman. The crew was a mixed bunch of Africans and Europeans. Harry loved this mix, he wanted to learn from as many nationalities as he could. Onboard ship, he had the time and the patience to absorb the language. Sara had the same time but a better appreciation of the important features of the language.

Sailing out of Cape Town Bay was spectacular and they were heading north to Walvis Bay. Sara said goodbye to Table Mountain and hoped she would come back. The captain informed them they could expect some rough weather. True to his prediction, the sea was pretty rough and they stayed in their cabin most of the day. The cabin had a double bed, a toilet, shower and two portholes. The next two days were rough and meals were small and slowly eaten. On the third day, they joined the captain for dinner. The captain was from Newcastle in the north of England, Sara listened to his accent intensely. It was so different to Harry's.

"We get very few passengers on this route and I think you are the first going to Lagos. Do you have some reason to go there?"

"Yes, my uncle has a business and he is getting old, so we're going to help him."

"Lagos is a growing city with plenty of trade. They seem to like goods from Europe rather than South Africa. We unload about twice as much when we come from England, as we do coming from South Africa. Our crew is a mixed bunch, we have a couple of Nigerians, two from the Gold Coast, an Irish first mate, a Portuguese navigator and a few Arab sailors."

The captain did not realise Sara was an Arab and she did not enlighten him. Harry was interested to talk to all of them, particularly the navigator, as they would be visiting Angola. Sara asked a few questions about Newcastle but the captain still did not realise she wasn't English.

The captain explained that they did not stop at many ports below the equator as trade was difficult with some of the French territories and the Belgian Congo. The Portuguese were much friendlier and accustomed to trade, so after Walvis Bay they would go to Luanda then Sao Tome and Principe (we call it Saint Thomas and the Prince). Most of the trade was carried out along the Bight of Benin and then along the North African coast. Lagos, Accra, Abidjan and Freetown are the main trading ports.

"At this time, goods from South Africa sell better in Abidjan and Freetown." The captain foresaw that, in the future, Accra and Lagos would be the most profitable ports.

Harry had plenty of time to chat with the navigator and pick up some Portuguese words and phrases. They discussed Lourenço Marques and the navigator, Fabio, told Harry that Luanda would be friendlier. If the captain would let him go ashore, he would accompany Harry and Sara. They would see a very different city to Lourenço Marques.

Sara found a few of the Arab sailors and one was Iraqi, although his parents now lived in Lebanon. He was so shocked when she spoke to him in his native tongue, he was speechless, he thought she was English. All the Arab sailors crowded around as she addressed them in Arabic, throwing in a few phrases for the Egyptians. They all started to clap and cheer and the captain shouted from the wheel house.

"It's okay, captain. I'm telling them some jokes."

Now the captain was speechless.

"I thought your wife was English," he said to Harry.

"Her English is pretty good, her Arabic is excellent, but her Swahili needs work. She is actually Iraqi-Sudanese. Don't worry, captain, she will have them eating out of her hand. She has a way with people, she fools so many."

The captain agreed she had fooled him.

Neither of the Nigerians was from Lagos but they were Yoruba and the two from the Gold Coast were also related to the Yoruba. The Nigerians explained that in the country the chiefs had control, but in Lagos the

130

British had control; hence, there was little control. There was a continual human flow to Lagos, where people thought they could make easy money. Both Nigerians agreed that they could never live in Lagos, it was too dirty and crowded. The sailors from the Gold Coast said more or less the same about Accra. They were all saving money to build a house in their village and pay the dowry for a wife. One of them explained that if you wanted to choose a wife, you paid the dowry but you could get one when her family paid the dowry. They all laughed. All four agreed that when they had earned enough money, they would live far away from the sea and the big city.

As they approached their next port, all the sailors became excited. Walvis Bay had a very orderly dock. This was South West Africa run by the South Africans. The town was very regulated, the streets were well planned and many of the houses were very European in look. Only a few of the crew would leave the ship, they were wary of the South African police. Harry and Sara disembarked and had no problem with the authorities. Harry often thought it could be different if Sara had a Sudanese or Iraqi passport. There were people of all colours on the street but it was quiet. There was little traffic. They walked for a while until they saw a restaurant — a German restaurant run by South Africans — and they decided to eat there. Harry was able to drink the best beer he had tasted on this trip. Sara detected a different accent to Durban or Cape Town.

She loved hearing different sounds, it had probably developed from Harry's speech. The restaurant staff were friendly but not over friendly. Both Harry and Sara felt that they were being watched, so it was a relief to get back to the ship.

The priority on leaving Walvis Bay was to learn some Portuguese. Harry was priming the captain to let Fabio take them into Luanda. The captain was amused by this couple talking all sorts of languages, but he was glad he had a happy crew. Even the Irishman was entering into the comradery. He tried a bit of Gaelic but had no response.

As Luanda approached, Fabio became excited. On this trip there were only two places he felt at home, Luanda and Sao Tome. "I can walk into town and feel I'm at home. My home is Oporto."

"I was supposed to stop at Oporto on my journey to Sudan," mentioned Harry, "but there wasn't enough cargo to pick up."

"You missed some good wine and *jamon* (ham). They smoke the leg and cut slices and put them on fresh bread. It's so delicious with wine. We'll try it in Luanda. If they have good sardines we'll try them, too. My mouth is already watering."

Sara was now teaching the Arabs to read and write, having smuggled more paper into her luggage. The captain had a happy crew, and when he barked orders, they all did as they were told. Harry's Portuguese was coming along and he was also learning about the West African Coast. The weather was good and the sea very calm and the crew had more time to talk. One day they went on deck and saw a huge whale, not more than twenty feet from the ship. They were spellbound. The mate came and told them there was a school of whales on the port side. They had seen flying fish off the Kenyan Coast and some smaller fish off Cape Town but this was astonishing. All morning this school followed the ship. They seemed to be playing with the vessel. Sara kept asking how long these whales were.

"This compares with the fish on the reef off Port Sudan. I must write to my sisters but where can I post a letter?"

"I think we have to wait until Lagos," said Harry. "We have to send letters to my parents, your parents, Abdul and Sami. Maybe we should take an afternoon and relax, writing letters."

"How do you write about this experience? This is truly wonderful," Sara sighed.

"Letters can never capture this experience. Only telling the story will be good enough but I think it will be many years before we can tell this story.'

They had been so involved with the crew, even Sara had forgotten her diary. The captain lost his companion and the crew lost their teacher for one afternoon. This afternoon was magical. They both started to recognise they were loving language; the words, the sounds and the meanings. That was hard to put into letters but hugging each other, they realised that they loved each other and loved what each other loved.

As they sailed into Luanda, they saw this was a different port, more like Mombasa. There was less order and lots of noise. Luanda was very different to Lourenço Marques, the streets were filled with Africans and Portuguese. Some of the shops were run by Africans and although the hotel was run by Portuguese, the staff were mainly African. Fabio was in an excited mood and ordered too many dishes. The sardines in a hot sauce were the favourites and the prawns were so good, Harry asked for more. Fabio took a long time to choose the wine, he wanted Harry to get the best to go with the seafood. Sara had a pineapple juice and loved it. Fabio wouldn't let them pay and promised they could pay in Sao Tomé. As they left the hotel, Fabio was almost dancing and as they approached the ship, he said, "I generally go ashore alone and probably get drunk but I'm sober and have had the best time of my life."

The next voyage was to Sao Tomé; a long journey mainly out of sight of land, presenting a good time to catch up on languages. Sara and Harry found out that Yoruba was a tonal language and sounds and expressions were important. *Oibo* meant white man or peeled skin. The way it was said was important, if said with a smile and in a sing-song way, it was good but if said with a frown and going down on the last *o*, it wasn't nice. Similar words could have different meanings and it was important to see the expression on the speaker's face. Sara and Harry nodded their heads at these rules. Could they conquer this language?

Fabio was so excited as they approached Sao Tomé, he was singing a song no one on the ship knew. This was a small port but there was plenty of activity.

"I smell cocoa," Sara said.

"Yes," Fabio replied. "That's their major export."

There was no problem with disembarkation and Fabio showed them around the town. While walking up a cobbled street, Harry had memories of streets in Ladywood that were cobbled. He now started to think of his childhood and how carefree life was while he was at school. He always looked up to his father but the last time they met, that spirit had gone, all due to the treatment of Jacob. His father had become more like the father who said NO to Ari, asking to take a daughter out. He looked back on it knowing he wouldn't have met Sara, but rejection left a bad taste.

Fabio seemed to be well known in the town and there were many greetings from the shop owners. At one coffee shop, a rather large woman came out and wrapped her arms around Fabio.

"This is Moma Roza," he smiled. "She makes the best spicy coffee."

They sat and had a coffee and it was spicy. Sara asked for a glass of water and Roza laughed. At lunch time, they went to a fish restaurant where the sardines were described by Fabio as being the best on the island.

135

The wine was from Portugal as the tropical climate on the island wasn't very good for growing wine grapes. Fabio let Harry pay but said he had to buy the port as it was his national drink. They had to walk to a bar where he said they had the best variety of old port. He admitted that he would have had several drinks in this bar but today he would only have one.

After the port (Sara just had water), they retreated to the wharf, the humid climate made them sleepy. On the wharf they met some of the crew supervising the loading of the cargo. Harry asked what was being loaded. The main commodities were cocoa and palm oil. Fabio explained that there would be very few other items and nothing edible. He loved this island but feared for its future. The evening meal on the ship was fish but not sardines. The cook had obtained some sea shark from a local fisherman, and grilled it, the taste was delicious. The only complaint was that Harry had not been able to use his Portuguese on the island.

"I'm sorry, Harry, but when I'm in Birmingham or Khartoum, I'll let you do all the talking as I'm sure they will not understand a word I say."

Sara couldn't stop laughing, this she thought very amusing. Harry had to laugh. If his wife found it funny, then he had to agree.

"You are more likely to catch me in Lagos, where I'm intending to stay for a few years."

Sara was in a good mood. "Next time you are in Lagos, come to visit us," she suggested. "Just ask for an

Englishman who is hard to understand, with a good-looking wife."

"I think my wife is acquiring my sense of humour."

The captain, the first mate and Fabio were all laughing at Harry.

Next stop was Duala in the Cameroon. Harry and Sara were talking to the Nigerians as much as they could without disturbing their work. The Nigerians emphasised that when two people met there would be a series of greetings and that could depend on what had happened recently. If a father had died, there would be a specific greeting; if a mother was sick, there would be a different greeting. If two strangers met, they would ask after the health of the person and the family, greetings could go on for an extended period.

The captain was marvelling at his passengers. They kept the whole crew happy. Normally there would be a few squabbles, which he would have to settle but this was a very easy crew. He was wondering if the same camaraderie would be kept up after Lagos.

Fabio said that he wouldn't be able to accompany Harry and Sara ashore as the captain and first mate had to talk to the agent. They were thinking of not stopping at Duala until trade picked up. These ships depended heavily on moving as much cargo in and out of a port and at present, trade in Duala was slow. Fabio advised that in Duala the predominant language was French but English should be understood. He suggested Harry and Sara should take a look at this city, it had some interesting architecture and some intriguing sounds and smells. Fabio realised that this couple loved sounds and smells.

As soon as they landed, the French influence was everywhere. Customs and Immigration was manned by French officers, the bakery was French, the bread smelt delicious and most of the signs on the shops were in French. They wandered through the town and found the Post Office in French and English, but the laundry seemed to be in English.

"English keep it clean and French do everything else," Harry laughed to Sara.

It was hot and humid and they soon decided they needed a rest. They entered a café and Sara ordered two coffees. She thought to order in her schoolgirl French but decided on English. As soon as she ordered, a man at the next table asked her what part of England she was from. She replied, "Khartoum."

The man frowned.

Harry spoke up. "My wife is Iraqi-Sudanese and I am from Birmingham."

"I'm Harry, the British Consul here. Your wife had me fooled. I was trying to work out her accent."

"That's a coincidence, I'm also Harry."

"What are you doing in Duala?"

"We're passing through on our way to Lagos. We've come from Sudan, by sea."

"What a journey! This is my first posting in Africa and I want to see more. The only problem with this place is the heat and humidity."

"Try Khartoum, it is hot but rarely humid. The only problem is that it is far from the sea. My wife and I have come to love the sea. This is an interesting city. Do you speak French?"

"Yes, but out in the town the French is more like a creole and of course, everything in the High Commission is in English. I must get back to work but if you're staying for lunch, there's a small hotel called the Meridien. I recommend it. I was glad to meet you both and madam has shown me not to jump to conclusions."

Harry turned to Sara. "What is creole?"

"I don't know. We should ask the captain."

They wandered around the town and saw lots of European-style buildings. The most interesting place was the market, where the stallholders spoke in the native language and French, but could also converse in a crude form of English if asked a question. Sara enjoyed this back and forth with language and was renewing her interest in French. She little realised this was a French patois. The Meridien had an excellent restaurant with fillet mignon and French wine. Harry was coming to love wine but Sara still drank fruit juice or a soft drink. One thing Sara enjoyed was the variety of sweets, Harry called these puddings. He did not have a sweet tooth but his wife did. After their meal, they strolled for a while and seemed to be greeted in various languages. Harry tried Arabic and Swahili to much amusement, until one man responded in Arabic.

"I'm Lebanese and own a shop here."

"How is business and are you the only Arab here?"

"Business could be better but we survive. There are many Arabs, particularly Lebanese, along the coast but you'll find more in Lagos."

"That's where we are going, we've come from Khartoum."

"*Al Hamdu llilah*, may you find your fortune there. I thought your sound was Egyptian but I don't hear my language often enough to pick accents."

"I had a shop in Khartoum. Tell me more about the business here."

"Not so good. My best sellers are coffee, dried fruit and corned beef. I was lucky to get tinned honey and treacle from one ship and that sold out very quickly but these things are hard to get as fewer ships seem to be coming to Duala."

"Yes, I understand the ship we are on may not come here till trade picks up."

They left the Lebanese shop owner a little bit more depressed.

Back on board, there was a problem, one of the Gold Coast sailors had got lost. His friend said they had parted in a bar when his friend had been attracted to a woman. The captain was annoyed but said he would delay sailing for a couple of hours in the morning. Early in the morning, a battered sailor was delivered to the ship. He had been beaten and robbed but they did not take his identification. The captain addressed the whole crew and warned them they could be left in a foreign port if they couldn't report back to the ship; they should stay in twos when ashore and avoid prostitutes and strong liquor. Sara was in full agreement with the captain. Harry added that every port was a trap for the unwary. He wanted them all to see England but they should each be careful. The whole crew clapped his speech.

Lagos

From Duala, the ship followed the coastline, it was all trees with a few beaches. As the ship entered Lagos Port, both Harry and Sara were excited. This was a large port with many ships and lots of small local craft. They had a pilot and docking the ship was tricky. The captain and the crew all stood as one to wish Sara and Harry good fortune, many of the crew wished their passengers could stay on board till Tilbury.

As they entered Lagos harbour, Fabio was almost in tears. He was trying to tell Harry and Sara that this was the best trip he had ever experienced along this coast. There were many handshakes as they disembarked and the captain said they were the best passengers he had ever entertained — or maybe they had entertained him.

Clearing customs should have been easy but one bag contained twisted cheese. Sara explained it was goats' cheese from the Sudan. None of the local officers knew where Sudan was, so she ate a piece and offered a piece to them. They all retreated and called over a white officer. He looked at it, smelled it and tasted it. Harry intervened and said they were from Khartoum, where this was the common cheese. Then he said General

Gordon would have eaten this cheese and the officer laughingly replied he thought the cheese was old. Problem solved.

Walking outside the gate, they were greeted by two men. Harry walked up and hugged Simon. They kissed and then Harry introduced Sara. Simon and Sara shook hands and then Simon introduced George. George was a small, rather fat, balding Nigerian with a fantastic smile.

"George is not a very Yoruba name. I assume you are Yoruba," ventured Harry.

"My mother loved Queen Victoria, so my eldest brother is Edward, I'm George, my next brother is Arthur and my youngest brother is Henry. We have two sisters, Victoria and Charlotte. Of course, we all have Yoruba names but all except Henry prefer to use their English names."

Sara approached George and addressed him in Yoruba with a couple of greetings. George stood back open-mouthed, and Simon said, "I'm shocked, surprised and delighted. This lady will take Lagos by storm. Where did you learn Yoruba?"

"Uncle, there were a couple of Nigerian sailors on our ship."

George was still shaking his head as they proceeded to the transport. He organised the luggage while the rest took a taxi.

"There's a strong smell," Sara said to Harry.

Simon overheard. "That is the open sewers. I'll show you when we get home. I know that when you first get to Lagos it is shocking, but after a while you get used to it and there are many things in Lagos you get to overlook."

As they approached the shops, they could see there were two shops joined with a common roof. Entering the first shop, they saw it was similar to the store in Khartoum. Moving through the shop to the rear, they found there were three apartments at the back of the shop. One apartment had been reserved for Harry and Sara. Simon explained that the furnishing was basic but he could afford new furniture.

After a while, the luggage and George arrived, he was still in awe of Sara. George showed them the second shop. This was the tailor's shop, with three tailors and four sewing machines. Sara greeted each tailor and received only stunned silence. Finally, George spoke. He couldn't remember any white person speaking such good Yoruba and he apologised for his tailors, who were in shock. Harry was just beaming and staying silent. He was going to practice his Yoruba later as he was sure Sara was better at it.

Simon called them all into the back of his shop. He made everyone sit at a table and offered them wine. Sara took a soft drink and then Simon began to speak.

"I came from Germany just before the war. I found George and we set up a shop. I sent for my wife but the war had started. My wife was trapped in Germany and she finally died in a concentration camp."

This was all said in a way that had Sara in tears and Harry close to tears.

"I should have brought my wife with me but Lagos was an unknown and I was afraid for her. I blame myself and I have never remarried. George is my companion, my partner, and his family is my family. I tell you this because I want to let you know the situation and being a relative you have allowed me to get it all off my chest. I'm a Jew but I do not go to the synagogue and I mix very little with other Jews. Lagos has a very mixed population but I do not go out of my way to mix with other Europeans. In business, I must mix with other nationalities but not socially. I'm known as a loner and I don't mind."

"You remind me of my Uncle Jacob. I'm here to help you and you're the boss," smiled Harry. "I don't go to the synagogue and my wife is Christian — and by the way, she is Iraqi-Sudanese. I want to know how this partnership works."

George now entered into the conversation. "I'm a tailor and when Simon and I met, I used to do tailoring from my home. Simon bought a shop, and I did tailoring in the back room. The next shop became vacant and we bought it. Simon put in most of the money but it allowed me to employ a couple of other tailors. Most of my clients are men but lately, some women are coming to us. It appears that some women want men's-style clothing. Maybe madam could help."

"That sounds interesting," responded Sara. "I'm feeling the humidity and would love to design women's clothing that is loose but elegant. I want to be a working woman and tailoring appeals to me. I'm very keen to support my husband and his family and their partners."

Sara now realised she had a role in this venture and she was pleased, she could be a working wife.

"Well, Uncle Simon, we seem to have a team. What problems do you have?" said Harry.

"Doing business in Lagos is always a problem but we need to have presence on the docks. I know our agent is coming under pressure. There are some people who know I'm a Jew and since the Palestine crisis, they are giving him problems. These people are Egyptians; they are putting pressure on my agent at the port. They want him to stop helping me."

"Don't worry, Uncle. I speak their kind of Arabic and will sort them out. In fact, I look forward to giving them a fright."

Simon then produced a bottle of brandy and toasted a new future. Harry asked about wine and liquor, he thought that the trade might be lucrative. Simon said that liquor was difficult, as that which was available was mostly smuggled; the brandy they were drinking was bought on the beach. Most Nigerians did not drink wine and if they did, it was sweet wine. Harry was thinking of Portuguese wine, some of it was semi-sweet. He would put that in his memory bank for the future.

Their flat behind the store was adequate and Sara was able to make it comfortable. Harry wanted to see the surrounding area, so they went for a walk. There were a few stares and when Harry gave a greeting in Yoruba, the stares turned to laughter. Sara told Harry that next time, she would reply. The stares turned to surprise and Sara told Harry his accent might not be quite right. Harry was always amazed at Sara, she was better at almost anything.

The next day, Harry went to the British High Commission to make sure their visas were in order, he had a plan for the Egyptians. He submitted the passports and within a few minutes he was summoned to see the consul.

"I have heard a lot about you from the consul in Khartoum, who is my friend, and now the consul in Duala. I understand you have a good knowledge of Arabic and it is possible that might be useful to us. Lagos has many nationalities and we have to watch that there is no funny business."

"Thank you. I'll be glad to be of service. Call on me any time you wish. By the way, I know a bit of Yoruba."

"How long do you wish to stay?"

"Indefinitely."

"That is okay but we may find that Nigeria will gain independence in a few years."

"I hope to be well established before then and also hope we have many meetings, unless you get posted elsewhere."

"My wife would love that, but I think we'll be here for a while."

"I'm sure my wife would like to meet your wife some time."

"Yes, the consul in Duala says your wife is quite a lady."

They parted with a handshake and Harry left the building in a very good mood. Things had worked out much better than he had planned. He was now in a position to tackle the Egyptians. He had to talk to the shipping agent on the dock and as it was quite a walk, he decided to take a taxi. The driver was amazed at his Yoruba and only found a few tonal mistakes. Harry was going to use any chance to improve his Yoruba. He was starting to enjoy Lagos, the heat humidity and smells had all become bearable.

He found the agent's office and introduced himself. The agent was from the north of England and worked through a firm that had agents all along the West African Coast. He confided in Harry that he was being pressured by a couple of his Egyptian clients to ditch Uncle Simon as a client. Harry said he would deal with them and asked when the agent expected to see them again.

"I think they'll come tomorrow morning as they have goods to clear."

"I'll be here early tomorrow morning and we can chat about anything you like. If you're busy, I'll sit quietly in the corner. By the way, how long have you been here?"

"Six years. My wife left after two, she couldn't stand the heat and the smells."

"Why do you stay?"

"I'm waiting for a better posting and with this job I get a good holiday allowance."

Harry was enjoying this and when he returned to his new home, he was in a very jovial mood. Sara was also in a very good mood, she had spent most of the day with George in his workshop. He had three tailors working with him and they were amazed at Sara's Yoruba. She had learnt some new phrases but more importantly, she had watched them work, cutting and stitching the cloth. George had explained that most of their customers were male but they occasionally had a female customer who just wanted some stitching or adjustment. Sara had an idea, she wanted to design European style clothing for women. Because of the heat and humidity, it had to be loose but stylish. She needed a mannequin and George's help to make a sample. George was very keen but had no idea where to buy a mannequin. Sara told George not to worry, she would order one from London.

The next day, Harry was in the agent's office bright and early, firstly ordering two female mannequins from London. As they were having coffee, the agent saw the two Egyptian merchants approaching his office. Harry smiled. Now for some fun. The two merchants entered the office chatting in Arabic and then approached the agent.

"We are here to collect our goods but we'll withdraw our custom unless you get rid of this Simon."

"Let me introduce myself. I'm Simon's nephew. I'm here taking charge of his business. We'll increase our business with this agent and he might not need your trade."

The couple looked at each other and said something in Arabic.

"I'll now speak to you in your tongue as I do not want to embarrass this Englishman. Your businesses may or may not be totally legal, a simple investigation of the visas of you and your employees could be initiated soon. Then your tax situation may also come under scrutiny. The other day I was talking to the consul and my knowledge of Arabic may be useful to them. I look forward to seeing you in the future. I hope you understand what I'm saying. I was thinking your stay in Lagos may not be long."

The two men quickly retreated from the office and the agent asked what had happened.

"I warned them off. I'm very versed in Arabic and have put them on notice that they're being watched. Knowing this kind of Egyptian, there is probably something to hide. Thank you for your time and the use of your office, it has given me great pleasure."

The taxi drive back to Simon's shop gave Harry another opportunity to practice his Yoruba. This driver did not seem surprised at Harry's efforts; nor did he try to correct his sentences. Word must have spread very quickly amongst the taxi drivers.

Harry started to look at Simon's shop and decided, amongst other things, that they needed a cold room. At present, ice blocks were delivered from the factory, Harry was amazed to see an ice block on the head of a cyclist who was delivering it to the shop. He sat down with Simon to discuss some changes but Simon wasn't convinced, he had done business his way for years. A cold room and air conditioning for the living quarters was going to cost a lot of money. Harry said not to worry as he had transferred money to England from Sudan and after opening an account in Lagos, he would finance the project with funds from England. Simon smiled and thought to himself that if Harry wanted to waste English pounds, he wouldn't stand in his way.

Over the next few weeks, Harry spent a lot of time rearranging the shop. He found he was quite tired at the end of the day and Simon told him to slow down, the humidity was the problem. Sara spent all her time learning to cut and sew cloth. She was doing no real physical work but she was tired in the evening. Harry was wishing for the air conditioning so they could resume their nightly manoeuvres. Sara put some of her clothes on a hanger in the shop in a prominent position.

She asked Harry to see who was looking at the clothing as she spent her time with the tailors. Most of the customers in the shop were male but one or two women started to look at the garments. Sara was telling Harry that as soon as the mannequins arrived, she would put one in the shop and one in the tailor's workshop. Harry was so in love with his wife that if she had asked him to send one to the moon, he would have agreed. He did notice more women were coming to the shop. Sara would rearrange the clothes every day and a couple of the women showed a great interest in the dresses.

Sara thought things were going too slowly, so one Sunday she decided to go to church. Harry apologised and sat outside. The congregation was mixed and Sara noticed a few well-dressed white women. Most of the Nigerian women were dressed traditionally and Sara could see the quality of their clothes. Sara sat near the middle of the church so that the ladies in the front would see her when they left the church, she assumed they were potential clients. She was in a loose dress with a small sleeveless jacket. A couple of ladies, one white and one Nigerian, came after the service to admire her attire. They asked where she bought her clothes and were surprised when she said she made her outfit in her uncle's shop. This was what she was waiting for, but she decided to be patient.

After two days, the Nigerian lady from the church came to the tailor's shop. She looked at Sara and looked at one of Sara's suits on a hanger. She bounced around the shop and said, "Can you make me something like that?"

Sara answered in Yoruba. "Yes. I'll have to take measurements and discuss how it will fit."

The woman was so shocked, she was speechless for a minute. George and the tailors wanted to laugh but they were also speechless.

"Where did you learn to speak our language? I have never heard a white person speak it so beautifully."

"I learnt a lot on a boat and my boss, George, and his staff have taught me a lot of useful phrases. We have a good working team here."

All the tailors were beaming when Sara praised them. George was standing in the background and heard what had been said. He wanted to say something but he restrained himself. After all the measurements and discussion about style, the Nigerian lady left and George had to speak.

"I'm not your boss."

"Maybe I should have said tutor, but I couldn't think of the word. As long as you run this shop, you are my boss."

The tailors were talking excitedly. They wanted to know who this client was. Sara explained she would find out when she made out the receipt. She was amused at their reaction and told Harry later.

Within two days, the lady returned for a fitting. They had to rig up a curtain and Sara decided they should have a fitting room. She was now in a new situation, there had to be a few minor alterations but the lady wanted to take it straightaway. Sara said that they would do it immediately.

"I'm coming back this afternoon. I want to wear this tomorrow."

George laughed. "When these women want something, do not stand in their way. Can you fix it in two hours?"

"Yes, they are only minor changes and now she knows I'm taking my time to do the best for her, she will be back for a second dress in the future."

"That is very clever," smiled George.

"You must let your customer know they are very important. It is more vital with females."

Harry wanted to let Uncle Simon have his way but he thought there was need for some changes. The cold room was going to change a lot of the stock but there was a great deal of old stock that needed clearing. Harry decided to go to the local market and talk to the stallholders. He found they were mostly women and when he talked to them in Yoruba, he soon gathered a crowd. He told them he would bring some items to the market and whatever they bid, he would accept the price. He was conducting an auction, which had never happened before. The crowd was still marvelling at his Yoruba when he left.

The next day he made his way to the market, arriving with some of the old stock, and stood on a packing case. He told the audience (in Yoruba) how an auction worked and there was complete silence while he spoke. This was the quietest market in Nigeria. The first item was going to be a guide to how the auction would go. He held up a small statue of Queen Victoria, knowing that the market mommas in the market wouldn't sell it. The first bid was from a man and then the mommas took over. This item went for much more than it was worth and the lady who bought it stood up and raised the statue, so everyone could see. The audience cheered and clapped and a few offered her more than was paid.

Most of the other items went for more than they were worth. There was no problem in the audience and everything went more smoothly than Harry could have imagined. After the last item sold, he made a speech. He said that three ladies had done most of the bidding and he had a small present for them. He presented each of them with a necklace and the crowd was cheering. The ladies were almost in tears and they all hugged Harry. He spoke again and hoped that they had all enjoyed a morning of entertainment and he would be back again soon. Harry had made more in a day than the shop made in a week. On his way home, he decided not to tell Uncle Simon how much he had made.

Sara was talking to George when the Nigerian lady bounced into the shop.

"My husband looked at me this morning like he has not looked at me for years! I want another suit. This time, I want trousers. I think you might get more custom but I'm priority."

"If you want trousers," replied Sara, "we need to take a few more measurements. Did your other suit fit well?"

"I tell you, I have never had any clothing fit so well."

After she left the shop, George said, "You have opened a door that will be hard to close."

The receipt revealed the lady's name and all the tailors wanted to know who she was. Sara was a bit amused but George explained that they would go home and try to find out what they could about her. They would want to know about her family, her husband and his family. They would want to know their origins. Most people in Lagos were from somewhere else. He was fourth generation Lagotian, his great-grandfather had settled here. George did not know where he came from but assumed it was close to Lagos. The female line was unknown but he did know his mother came from Cotonou (Benin). Two of the tailors came from near Ibadan and one was second-generation Lagotian.

"If I meet another Yoruba I do not know, we'll have greetings and ask about our families but towards the end, we want to know where we are from."

"George — we are the same," agreed Sara, "but maybe we come out with the question 'Where are you from?' earlier."

They both laughed at the similarities. This had been a good day.

Sara knew this project might become big and warned George to plan for more custom. The other tailors were aghast, they had never heard a Nigerian woman talk like this. Sara decided that it was time to meet some other expatriate ladies. She asked Harry to take her first to the High Commission and then to the Victoria Hotel for lunch. Harry could never say no, but he knew Sara had some scheme.

At the High Commission, she met the consul and then was introduced to the High Commissioner. They were enthralled by her story and astonished by her English (her beauty probably had some effect). As they left the High Commission, Sara said it had been a good morning.

At the Victoria Hotel, the staff were amazed when she told them, in Yoruba, what she wanted. She suspected one of the staff was Arab, so she asked him the time of day. He looked at her.

"Iraqi?" he asked.

"How did you know?"

"I'm Iraqi and something in your voice sounded familiar."

The head waiter came over and asked if there was a problem. Harry told him relatives had met, half a world away. He added that when they came again, they wanted this waiter and then repeated it to the waiter in

Arabic. Some of the other patrons were looking, as Harry did not lower his voice.

The lunch was good and they chatted with the waiters and other diners. One Nigerian came to the table and asked how long they had been in Lagos. Harry replied in Yoruba. The man stood back and said he understood but he was Hausa from the north. Unfazed, Harry addressed him in Arabic. Now the man was almost speechless but he did say that Harry's Arabic was good and asked where he had learned the language. Harry told him Sudan. The man was muttering something to himself that Harry couldn't understand. Harry also told him he traded with the Bedouin, many had come through Northern Nigeria.

"In Lagos, you are something special. If you ever come to Kano, please look me up. Here is my card."

"Am I invited, too?" Sara said, in Arabic.

"I have never been asked that question by a woman. I'll have to ask my wives. You are an amazing couple. You'll both be welcome at my house, but I must be careful unless you give my wives too many ideas."

Sara had planned to be seen and that was what was happening. Everyone was staring and the northerner bent and kissed her hand. Again, Sara said their visit was successful.

The cool room was almost finished and the apartments' air conditioning was complete. Harry and Sara were feeling the benefits, bedtime was much more pleasant. They were also brighter in the morning and

even Simon was appreciating the conditions. Harry was planning on air conditioning the shops, but that would have to wait.

They had not been in Lagos for many weeks and they were being noticed. The tailor shop had become a hive of activity and George had to take on another tailor. It wasn't just the women's trade; more men were coming to the shop. Harry had asked Sara if she should slow down but she was enjoying being more than useful, she was making important decisions.

One day, an English lady came to the shop and wanted to look at some women's clothing. The mannequins had arrived and were displaying garments, one in each shop. Gladys was married to a Nigerian and admired the clothing but thought the mannequins too skinny for Lagos. After a long discussion about England, Gladys invited Sara to an afternoon tea where there would be some Nigerians and some European ladies. Gladys understood Sara spoke excellent Yoruba and was interested in the reaction of the women. Sara told Harry that this was just the kind of group she wanted to enter. She became a bit nervous but Harry suggested she tell them about Khartoum or her trip around the coast of Africa.

"You could even amuse them by talking about double-decker buses."

Gladys's group was a mixed bunch, three Nigerians, two English, one German and two

Americans. Sara introduced herself as an Iraqi Sudanese with an English husband. They had travelled around Africa to get to Lagos. The first question was from one of the Nigerian women.

"I understand you can speak Yoruba but how much do you know?"

"Excuse me, ladies. I'll now speak in Yoruba, much of which I learned onboard ship."

Sara then described her time in Lagos (in Yoruba), her clothes-making for the climate and her understanding of the importance of family and place of origin for Lagotians.

There was silence for a while and one of the other Nigerian ladies said that she was amazed and would love to hear that all again. The other ladies wanted to hear that in English. Sara was a hit. Gladys explained this group met every week and Sara was welcome any time, she thought she would attract more women. Sara agreed to come next week and talk about Khartoum. The next week the group had grown. Sara gave half her talk in Yoruba and half in English. She asked if anyone spoke Arabic but no one did. All the ladies marvelled at her language skills.

Harry had also made some Nigerian friends and had been invited to join a club where he would be the only white man. These were educated Nigerians who held discussions on all sorts of topics. Many of them had been to university in England and Harry wondered whether he could enjoy such company. He was asked to give a short talk on any subject. He decided to talk about Khartoum but gave the talk in Yoruba. It was a great success and they pleaded with him to give another talk, when he was ready. These men were doctors, lawyers and two were judges, many of them interested in politics and the Independence of Sudan. They were pushing for Independence, it was happening in Sudan and the Gold Coast was moving that way. Harry said he would try to get information from Khartoum through his father-in-law, but he couldn't be involved in politics. This group understood his problem and they all appreciated his position.

Everything was going well until Simon started to get sick. George said he had never known Simon to be unwell other than a bout of malaria. Harry realised he would need help if Simon had bouts of sickness. He discussed it with Sara and suggested they invite Paul, her youngest brother, to come to Lagos. They would pay his airfare. Harry was writing regularly to his father-in-law and thought he would sound him out first. The reply was that Paul missed his sister and so they would be happy to let him go. Simon recovered and Harry told him about Paul. Simon was so happy with Sara and what she had done, he had no problem with her brother coming to live in Lagos. George said if Sara's brother was anything like her, he would be very welcome.

They were getting ready to welcome Paul when Simon became sick again, this was serious. Sara and

George went to the airport while Harry found a doctor to examine Simon. Having done so, the doctor said he probably had pneumonia but not TB (a similar diagnosis to Jacob). Harry was looking at Simon and seeing Jacob. Simon wouldn't have his lungs drained but would take some pills. After taking four pills, he decided they did not work and would take no more. Harry was glad to welcome Paul but sad watching Simon fading away. Simon did brighten up when he saw Paul, he was so much like his sister, who Simon loved like a daughter. Sara tried to cheer Harry up but realised this was a repeat of Jacob's passing. Harry was taking it badly; he would often disappear for a morning, sitting on the dock and staring at the sea. He would sit and think about Jacob. Losing a wife and trekking to Khartoum, why did he not give up and leave Sudan? These were questions that repeated themselves. Why was he in Africa? He should have given up, but then he had met Sara and that was very good compensation.

When Jacob had been dying, Harry would often go and sit by the Nile, he couldn't deal with death. He had to think of the past. With Simon, he was thinking of his father's shop in Ladywood. He wanted Simon to live in a very organised place. Why had Simon stayed in this difficult city? The pain he must have suffered, losing his wife in a concentration camp... Harry found looking out to sea offered him a sort of comfort.

Finally, Simon died. The ceremony was conducted in the synagogue. This time Harry couldn't discern any bad words about Simon and he gave a generous donation to the Rabbi. Simon was buried in the Jewish cemetery in Yaba, not far from the lagoon. Harry and George were sad for a few days but they consoled each other and decided that life and business must go on, with the shops opening up again after two days. Harry had lost two uncles in very different places but they had both lived quite different lives to their relatives. Harry now realised he was doing the same. He was less of an adventurer than they had been, but he still regarded himself that way.

The reading of the will was a very emotional time. Simon left the tailor shop to George with half the profits to go to Sara — the daughter he never had. The shop was left to Harry but he had to take George as a partner in the business, otherwise he could only own one half of the shop, the other half going to George's wife and children. The building was to be jointly shared by Harry and George, although the deeds would be in George's name. George was happy to take on Harry as a partner and vice versa. Sara was crying because Simon had called her a daughter, her husband had done wonders for the shop and Sara had done so much for the tailor's shop. The ownership of the building was a wise move when Independence came to Nigeria.

Harry and Sara were becoming a popular couple. They were invited to all kinds of functions, including wakes. They understood the Yoruba tradition and their hosts were delighted that they came to such events. Most parties were multicultural occasions but some of the dinner parties were not, the newly-weds fitted in at all the events. Their language skills were their greatest asset. Their Arabic was less useful but occasionally it was required. At one of the parties, an Arab guest asked Harry where he learned his Arabic — in the streets of Cairo? This was said in a sarcastic way, so Harry replied, first in English and then in Arabic, "No, in the streets of Khartoum." Harry suspected that his antagonist had been put up to it by a couple of Egyptians. They were still using the same agent, so he had not scared them off completely.

At another party, a lady came to Sara and said, "I buy my clothes in Europe."

Sara's reply was, "I hope your designers and tailors understand the heat and humidity in Lagos."

As with all successful people, there was an element of envy, but Harry's Yoruba friends showed no such emotions and Gladys's group showed no such feelings to Sara. A couple of Gladys's ladies were married to Harry's friends and they regularly met, as couples.

Paul was spending a lot of time with George's family, learning Yoruba. It seemed he had the same language skills as Sara. He was a handsome boy and George's wife had to fight off lots of interested girls. In the shop, he was an attraction and it seemed he had lots of admirers. Harry was at a bit of a loss how to advise him, so he asked Sara.

"Although I'm his elder sister, I cannot tell him what to do. In our culture, only an elder brother can give him advice he should follow. You are his elder brother, so he must listen to you. Be careful — he is a sensitive boy and I expect he is missing Khartoum but I'm sure Popa told him to give Lagos time."

"I never had a brother or sister, but funnily enough I thought of Sami as a brother. I wasn't thinking of Paul in the same way, maybe because of the difference in age. I should come to you with all my problems." They laughed, hugged and kissed.

"If that is my reward, you can solve all my problems," Harry said, shaking his head.

Harry gave Paul advice similar to that which his own father gave him, when going to Sudan.

"You are here to work and all this will be yours at some stage. Have some fun, but look to the future. Lagos is a tough place but if you can stick it out, you'll find it is a good place to live. Your sister and I are enjoying living here."

Paul seemed to take the speech well and said he was also enjoying Lagos.

Coming towards Independence, Sara's dressmaking was taking off. All the women were looking forward to lots of parties and they needed stylish garments, as well as traditional clothing. Sara had to get some assistance, so she asked George if one of his daughters would help. George had never thought of one of his daughters entering the tailoring business and he was a bit apprehensive, but Sara cooled his nerves by saying any of his daughters who wanted to work should be allowed to do so and Sara would do her best to train them.

George's eldest daughter, Bimpe, was being trained by Sara, but she wasn't too good at the work and admitted to her father that she might have a problem with her eyes. George took her to an optician and substituted his second daughter, Ife. Ife was very suitable and picked up measuring and cutting very easily. George thanked Sara as he now knew his eldest daughter had glaucoma. Now all his children and his wife had their eyesight checked. George's wife was particularly grateful as she was getting the health of all her children checked.

Sara was showing Ife how to stitch the cut cloth when a very tall, slim lady walked into the shop. She looked around and saw the dressed mannequin.

"I want one of those outfits in black and white and another in green and black. I'm only here in Lagos for three days. Could you have them ready?"

"It is possible, we already have the pattern and all we need is your measurements and hopefully we have the colour green you want. By the way, where are you from? Your English is very good."

"I'm from Enugu and I'm Ibo. My English was acquired at boarding school in England, near a little place called Bewdley. You have probably not heard of that town."

"I have heard of it and I have been there. My husband took me on a double-decker bus and we spent a lot of time by the river. Everything was so green."

"That is unbelievable! I was told you may not be English but you speak just like an English woman. I can hardly believe you know Bewdley."

"I'm Iraqi-Sudanese but my husband is English. We came from Khartoum, by sea, to Lagos."

"Khartoum, Gordon and the Mahdi — they were part of my history lessons and I loved history. What a sea journey — I assume it was via Cape Town? I'm here to buy dresses and you have taken me back to school. This is magical."

Ife was standing, awaiting instructions, and all this was a mystery to her. She had the tape ready and Sara said to make the measurements while she chatted with a new friend. This lady was much taller and slimmer than others she had measured and she asked Sara to check. Azo and Sara laughed as they realised that Azo wasn't the dimensions of a normal Yoruba woman. Azo explained that come Independence, there would be lots of parties and in Enugu she would be a principal organiser. After the celebrations, Sara should come with her husband and Ife to Enugu. It was quite a long journey but well worth the effort.

Ife was bouncing up and down when she told George she had been invited to Enugu. George wasn't too keen but Sara said she would look after Ife. Ladies from Ibadan and outside Lagos were coming for dresses and suits for the Independence celebrations. Word had spread of a white tailor who spoke the local language. Gladys reported that she had heard many comments but the most common one was, 'I have a new husband — he looks at me differently in this dress.' Gladys would also need a new dress for the celebrations, her husband was a high-ranking civil servant. Gladys had made sure Sara and Harry would be invited to most of the official functions.

Nigerian Independence came in 1960 and there was much rejoicing. Many of the British administrators departed but there were plenty left to help the new government. The consul was still 'on seat' and many of Harry's friends had important positions. The transition for Harry was very smooth. He had a Nigerian partner and the building was in George's name, so registration wasn't a problem. Harry had no difficulty staying in Nigeria and carrying on business as usual.

The parties were endless and Sara and Ife were flat out filling orders. Ife was telling her father what they needed and George was shaking his head in amazement. He was being told by his second daughter what he should do. The other tailors were starting to chat with Ife; they had been shy, as her father was their boss. Now she was taking a lot of the decisions and they could see she was a good manager.

After a few weeks, Sara decided they needed a break. She persuaded Harry they should go to Enugu. Sara and Azo had struck up a friendship, not based on language but a love of England. They were taking Ife with them and would leave Paul in charge of the shop. Although Paul was happy to be in charge, he was unhappy to see Ife leave. Sara and Harry had not noticed the friendship between the two of them.

Harry had never driven so far, so they stopped at a hotel in Benin City run by one of Sara's customers. After a longer drive, they entered Enugu and were directed to Eugene's (Azo's husband) house. This was a big house, more like a mansion, and it was surrounded by cultivated fields, reminding both Sara and Harry of England. Eugene, wearing a pale green suit, came to greet them. Harry was taken aback by the suit colour but when Eugene started to speak, he recognised a well-educated man. Eugene explained that he would prefer to wear a more sombre colour but he was representing his tribe in front of important visitors.

They sat down to dinner and as soon as Azo mentioned Bewdley, Harry was relaxed and smiling. Eugene had been to England but mainly in London. He was interested in Khartoum and that set Harry off on one his favourite subjects. He had plenty of news about Sudan's Independence and the events that followed. Ife was fascinated by the talk and asked a few questions; one was about Sara's family. Sara quickly recognised that Ife was asking about Paul's family. Later in the evening, she mentioned to Harry that they were missing something — Paul and Ife.

The next day they had a tour of Eugene's estate. It was large and well kept, they grew several crops and there was a manager for each crop. Harry asked Eugene about the future of Nigeria.

"You have asked me a very tricky question. Firstly, Nigeria is a very rich country but a big country. Tribalism is a real problem here; how to keep them all satisfied. What Nigeria needs is a stable political system that will benefit all parts of the country. I think it's possible but if I were a betting man, I wouldn't put my money on it."

"When you say 'put my money on it,' you sound like an Englishman."

"Thanks for the compliment. Secretly, I would like to be an Englishman."

That conversation sealed Harry and Eugene as friends. Eugene said that they should drink to their friendship and Harry said that was also very English.

Meanwhile, Azo and Sara were discussing clothes, families and children. Sara was open and said they couldn't have children. Azo was surprised and said it was a very sad thing to hear.

"In Nigeria, children keep a man attached to a woman. Even Christians take second or even third wives. A childless woman can have a hard time. You must have a very loving man."

"I understand what you say, but Harry is different. He seems to accept things that others can't. He stayed in Khartoum when I'm sure other Englishmen would have run away. He took on my family as his own and gave us opportunities that maybe would have passed us by and he allowed me to guide him occasionally. I couldn't wish for a better husband and if I had married an Iraqi, I'm sure I would have been worse off. My father is a doctor and he examined us both and could find no reason for our problem, so we have learned to accept our fate. My younger brother lives with us and I'm sure he will have children we can adore."

The evening meal conversation was a mix of Nigeria, Sudan and England. Ife wasn't left out of the conversation as she believed that everyone was equal and should have their say, even women. That sparked a conversation about women in Nigeria that could have gone on for hours until Sara mentioned that they had to leave early in the morning.

The journey back to Lagos was uneventful but when they reached the shop, the greeting between Ife and Paul was very cordial. Sara nudged Harry and they both smiled. It looked as though they were both happy to see each other. Harry told George he had a very intelligent daughter and the visit to Enugu was enlightening for everyone.

Two years passed, Paul and Ife were openly courting. Harry was unsure of his father-in-law's reaction but Sara could see a very capable woman in Ife and hoped Paul was her match. Azo and Sara were great friends and Azo was now part of Gladys's group. Eugene was introduced to Harry's Yoruba Club and there were a lot of enlightening discussions. Harry and George's business was doing very well and Paul and Ife were running both shops.

One day, Harry and Paul were in the shop when there was a loud explosion. They rushed into the kitchen to find Sara lying on the floor with half of her scalp removed. Paul fainted and Harry had to rush out the back to vomit. George came running in and froze. He was followed by Ife, who called to one of the tailors to get a doctor. Ife helped Paul up and ushered him into the shop. She then went into the kitchen to find Harry on his knees, sobbing. Ife then ran to the church to get the priest. Sara was still lying in a position with her hands raised to her face as though she was trying to protect herself. There was plenty of blood but the rest of her body had no marks.

The doctor pronounced Sara dead and the priest said the last rites. The doctor explained that a piece of metal from the stove had sliced through the top of Sara's head. Death would have been instantaneous and she would probably have felt nothing.

The stove had not been used for some time and Sara was cooking a small goat for an Iraqi festival. She was using this big stove which was large enough to take the small goat. There had obviously been a slow gas leak with a build-up of gas, which ignited when Sara lit the match. Harry couldn't think straight, his wonderful, beautiful wife was gone. The explosion had been reported to the police. They came and the doctor explained what had happened. They were satisfied and soon left.

Ife took charge and told George and Paul to shut the shops, there could soon be a crowd of inquisitive people. She decided to leave Harry alone, while she waited for the ambulance to take Sara to the mortuary. Harry was almost in a trance and did not really sense that Sara had gone. Ife tried to get him to go to bed but he was immovable.

Ife realised that the immediate family were in a state of shock, so she contacted Eugene, who was in Lagos. The news was such a shock that when he told Azo, she just broke down. Eugene understood that Ife was asking for help. He knew he had no chance to calm his wife but he had to arrange the funeral. He contacted Gladys to try to find out how Sara could be buried in an ordinary manner. On the phone, Gladys was strong and composed but when the call stopped, she couldn't stop crying.

A group met with the priest and decided on a date and time. Harry had not been consulted and was told of the preparations after they had been made. Harry had stayed in his bedroom for days, taking only water. Finally, Ife pushed George and Paul to tell him the arrangements. All Harry would say was "German Bombers." Neither Paul or George understood, so they left.

The church was full. Harry had to be guided to the front pew by Paul and Ife. Many of the expatriate community, including many of the embassy staff, were present. The British High Commissioner left the speech to the consul, who knew Harry and Sara well. He related that everyone thought she was English, the consul in Dyala had made that mistake. Sara had been a linguist and a humanist and she could have had a position in any university in England. She chose to be a designer and a lot of the ladies there were wearing her creations. He finished by saying that Khartoum had given Lagos a treasure.

That final tribute stirred Harry into action. Harry had sat quietly with his head in his hands. He stood up and spoke one sentence and sat down again.

"We have come a long way and enjoyed the journey. We'll end this journey together." He then sat down.

George related how Sara had transformed the business from a simple tailor's shop to a proper clothes-designer's outfitters. Sara had told him that word some time ago. In fact, Sara told him many words, mainly in his language. His wife had commented that Sara spoke better Yoruba than they did.

That stirred Harry again.

"My wife loved language, a passion we both shared."

Harry sat down again and never spoke another word.

George finished his speech by saying that he would forever be in Sara's debt. She had found a problem with his eldest daughter's eyesight and made his second daughter into an excellent tailor.

Finally, Paul spoke about his sister and family, Harry started sobbing. Paul told how, when his sister said she was going to Lagos, he had objected. Now Harry was openly crying. Harry had transformed his family into a well-respected family in Khartoum and it was Sara that made it all happen. When Harry and Sara asked Paul to come to Lagos, he was so delighted and all his sisters and brothers were jealous. He wished the whole family could be here. At this point, Harry stood up and left the church. Paul cut his speech short, saying only that the family had been notified by telegram.

As they left the church, Harry was standing motionless outside and had to be helped into one of the cars.

The cemetery was crowded and Harry just knelt silently by the pit. Paul, Ife and George kept everyone at bay, saying Harry wanted to be alone. After returning home, Harry went straight to his bedroom with a bottle of water.

George, Paul and Ife sat together after the funeral, deciding what to do. Ife suggested they shut the shops for a couple of days to get Harry ready for well-wishers. Each morning, Paul and George would take Harry his breakfast and later came back to collect the less than half-eaten food. Harry wanted no lunch but did need more water. After two days, when the shops opened, Harry would leave in the morning and come back late in the afternoon. He spoke to no one.

Harry would go to the sea wall and sit for hours. All he could think of was Sara lying near the stove. He tried to cloud that memory by thinking of their travels, but the vision kept coming back. He tried walking but that was no good. Then he decided to visit his solicitor. This man hardly knew Harry or Sara and talking to him gave a bit of relief. Harry drew up a new will.

This went on for four days and on the fifth day, when George and Paul entered his bedroom, Harry was hanging from a beam. George and Paul stood in stunned silence for a minute or two and then Paul called Ife. A note by the bedside table said that he had lost everything worth living for, the light of his life had gone out. His will was on the table and he had left his share of the business to Paul.

Harry/Ari was 42.

Returning from war

Part 1

1945 was going to be a great year for Jeff. He was demobbed and could go home, following his five years in the army. Called up in 1939, he had to leave his wife and young daughter. He had a two-day leave after training and then he was off to France. He was part of the Expeditionary Force but wished he was anywhere but France. At Dunkirk, he was lucky to be picked up by a fishing boat from a beach and although the trip home was rough, he was glad to land in an English harbour.

There were eight men and a driver in a lorry heading into Dunkirk. The driver said he knew Dunkirk and would go around the back of the city and head south. The lorry was stopped at a checkpoint and the driver said he wanted to turn left; he had more men to pick up. No one was arguing and so they headed south. The city was totally devastated. They were all hoping the Germans had not reached the south beach before them. They arrived, dashed to an empty beach and as luck would have it, a fishing boat was coming in.

The boat wouldn't come close to the beach, so they waded out. One man said he couldn't swim but a young man came from the boat and helped him get aboard. The captain was anxious to get going, not wanting to be a stationary target for a Stuka. He explained he had been fishing and heard the call, and not wishing to get close to the large navy ships, he came south. When they landed in England, they were some of the first to arrive home. The captain said he was going back to pick up more survivors; Jeff quietly thought him mad.

Jeff and his mates were taken to Aldershot and he was thinking about some leave, but to his surprise he was off to Egypt. The commander explained that information regarding Dunkirk wasn't to get out to the 'ordinary people'; the sergeant explained to Jeff that, as he was a motor mechanic, he was needed in Egypt, they had some problems with vehicles in the desert. Jeff had visions of working in a garage in Cairo, but the reality was very different.

Everything was in chaos and the only piece of extra kit he received was a pair of shorts. He was sent to Portsmouth to embark on a destroyer. As he boarded, a sailor casually said, "You'll see some action now."

"I was at Dunkirk."

The sailor was dumbfounded. "How come they're sending you to Egypt? Didn't you get leave?"

"No. They think I'll be more useful to the army than to my family."

This sailor and Jeff became good friends during the voyage. They sailed almost straight to Cairo, by-passing Gibraltar. They heard that the British fleet had locked up the French fleet and some French ships had sunk. Jeff expressed his surprise that they were sinking allied shipping. His friend explained that they were trying to stop the Germans getting hold of the French fleet.

Disembarking at Cairo was like organised chaos. At the bottom of the gang plank was an officer.

"Name, rank and serial number. Do you speak Arabic?"

"No, sir."

"Stupid question. You hardly speak English."

"I speak MY kind of English, SIR."

"That is insubordination, soldier. I could have you on a charge."

"After Dunkirk, throw the book at me."

"Oh! Go to that sergeant over there, he'll tell you where you are going."

Jeff rarely became annoyed but that upper-class twit of an officer had impugned his Brummie accent. Dealing with the sergeant was easier, he was from the North of England. Jeff almost laughed when the sergeant asked him why he was in Egypt. His answer was, "Ask the army."

"You'll be billeted in a camp tonight. Pick up some more suitable clothing and you'll be driven to where you're needed."

179

The billet was a rather large tent with bunks, but Jeff had a good sleep. The next morning, they were all woken at dawn to parade outside, within thirty minutes. Jeff was thinking this was like the Expeditionary Force. Names were called out and his was one of the first. He was to collect his gear and go to a jeep with the letter 'T' prominently displayed. He now had a second pair of shorts and a pair of sandals. Jeff smiled at his new outfit. When he located his jeep, he found he was the only passenger and tried to talk to the driver.

"I'm sorry, mate, but I can't tell you where we're going except that it's in the desert. Best of luck. By the way, look after those sandals. They're highly prized." The driver was laughing.

Jeff could do nothing but look at the scenery. There was nothing but desert, no people and little vegetation. With all this sand, he could understand the difficulty with vehicles. The sand was continually blowing across the road, which did not have tarmac on long stretches. They arrived at their destination and Jeff was shocked to find a line-up of WW1 lorries. As he alighted from the jeep, a sergeant came forward and they saluted.

"We deliver food and munitions to the troops in the forward posts. We've been promised newer lorries but at present, we have to make do with what we have. We have nothing for two days, so I would have you look over our fleet."

"Do we have parts, or a workshop?'

The sergeant laughed. "No, we only have the desert, mate."

Jeff threw his kit into a tent and walked to the first lorry. In the jeep, he hadn't noticed the heat but now he realised he had to get into his shorts. Opening the bonnet of the first lorry, he saw sand everywhere. He asked the sergeant if they had a compressed-air pump. The sergeant apologised and produced a hand pump.

"How do you pump up flat lorry tyres?"

"There's lots of manpower and time."

Jeff sighed and blew some of the sand from the engine. He checked the spark plugs and points. This lorry wasn't in bad shape, after blowing out the air filter, it started first time and sounded good. After going through most of the fleet, Jeff was surprised that the majority of the lorries were in good shape but he couldn't look at the engines and the gear boxes. Jeff had thought most of the fleet would be wrecks, but they were well made and durable.

"There are two lorries that need some work. Where can I get parts?

"Not around here but after our next delivery, I can send you to Cairo."

No one was supposed to talk about location, but Jeff found they were near the Egypt-Libya border and the front positions were on the border. The trip to the front line was on desert paths, no tarmac in sight. The fleet of lorries made it and unloaded. Jeff had a chance to talk to the front-line troops and when they learned he was at Dunkirk, he was a celebrity. They were waiting to see if the Italian troops would make a move.

All the lorries made it back to camp and Jeff was starting to appreciate their resilience. It was obvious he would need parts but could there be any for these ancient lorries? He thought they had been made before 1914 but he wasn't sure.

"I need to go to Cairo to find parts for these lorries."

"I can let you go for three days and you can take this 'Gypto' boy with you. He speaks a bit of English. Beware of the bints in Cairo."

Jeff turned to Hassim. "What did he say?"

"Bint, in Arabic, is girl, but I think he meant women of low character."

"I don't need one of them — I have a wife."

"Do you have children?"

"Yes — one little daughter and I miss her very much."

It turned out that the Gypto boy spoke good English, he had attended an English school in Cairo. He had sort of joined the army and was being paid by the British army, but had no assigned position.

"I'm sorry, sir, I find your accent a bit difficult but I'll learn to understand it. Please be patient with me."

Jeff laughed. "Coming from you, that's a compliment. Thanks, son. I'll try to speak slowly but if you don't understand, please let me know."

Hashim did not quite understand but he nodded. The journey to Cairo was more interesting, Jeff drove and Hashim pointed out some things Jeff had missed on his way to the camp. Somehow, his eyes focused better and he was seeing many things he had missed. Arriving at Cairo, Hashim directed the way to the army compound. Jeff was starting to appreciate his help.

When they arrived at the quartermaster's office, Jeff had to join a queue. He had a letter from his captain to get local money to buy spare parts. The quartermaster laughed.

"You want cash to buy spare parts? That's a new one. I don't think I can authorise that."

"I had less trouble getting off Dunkirk beach."

"You were at Dunkirk?"

"Yes, sir (that word, Dunkirk, worked again). And for my troubles, I landed in the desert but it is safer than Dunkirk." Jeff explained that the lorries taking provisions to the troops at the front were of WW1 vintage and he had to see if the souk had any parts.

The quartermaster introduced Jeff to his commander, a colonel.

"You want cash to go to the souk to buy parts? This is very unusual. In fact, I can't remember it happening before. How are you going to negotiate in the souk?"

"I have my right-hand man. He is a young boy who went to an English school and he understands my English. He will do the negotiating; I'll identify the parts. By the way, can you give me low denomination notes and any small change you have."

"I'm not convinced this will work, but report to me when you return with the change and some sort of list of parts."

Off they went to the souk and Jeff couldn't believe what he was seeing. There were so many parts of the lorries under his supervision. Obviously, many lorries had been destroyed and had been salvaged by the locals. Jeff identified parts and left Hashim to negotiate the price. Hashim took a long time but as Jeff had no idea of the price, he paid whatever Hashim agreed. Jeff did nothing, as all the parts were delivered to the lorry. On an approximate conversion to pounds, shilling and pence, Jeff thought they had a very good deal.

On receiving his change and a list of parts, the commander thought they had an unbelievable deal.

"I want to meet your right-hand man."

"Yes, sir. I'll fetch him. He is just outside. He is young, so don't be too official with him."

The colonel was smiling, he had a soldier telling him to go easy. Hashim was very bashful but the commander shook his hand and praised him for doing a great service to the army. Jeff loved this little 'Gypto' getting praise from a senior officer. Next time he was called a Gypto, Jeff would correct them and point out he was praised by a colonel.

They had purchased two radiators, hoses and lots of parts, including a whole gear box and back axle. The only parts not available were tyres. Jeff was happy with the day's work, when the lorry started to make strange noises. They pulled over and Jeff had to open the bonnet. He pulled out his trusty hand pump and blew away some of the desert. After a clean and restarting the motor, everything seemed okay but as the lorry pulled forward, he realised that it might be the gear box causing problems. He stopped the lorry and as he was about to get underneath it, a jeep pulled up.

Jeff saluted and the officer asked whether he could help.

"No, sir. I think this lorry has gear box problems and I'll have to nurse it back to base."

"You are a Brummie. I'm from Worcester.'

"Good to meet another Midlander. If you are going near our camp, we supply things to the front line. Tell them I'll be back soon. I'll have to nurse this back to camp."

"I'm going to your camp to look at the facilities and transport."

"The transport is a fleet of WW1 lorries that are still running but maybe running out of time. They are well built but getting old. This lorry will need a gear box change, and although I have a spare in the back, changing it will be a problem. I have no pit and I'll have to jack the lorry up. This desert ground isn't very stable. I'll work it out but after jacking it up, I'll have to climb underneath. I'm scared but I wouldn't let anyone else do it."

"That's a good line, I'll give to a politician I know. Can I be of help?"

"No, sir. I'll see you later."

Hashim was enthralled by the conversation. Here was a senior officer talking to Jeff like friends. Jeff nursed the lorry back to base and had the soldiers unload what he had bought. He reacquainted himself with the major and gave him a tour of the fleet.

"I'm told you were at Dunkirk. How come you are in Egypt so quickly?"

Jeff narrated his story and added that, so far, Dunkirk had been the magic word. If he used it, people became friendlier and things happened more quickly. The major laughed and told Jeff to keep using the 'magic' word. The major was full of praise for the little boats that rescued men from the beach. Jeff was hoping his saviour had come back from the second trip alive.

Within two days, Jeff was promoted to corporal and received a commendation which would later result in a medal. The gear box change was the hardest day's work Jeff had experienced. Most of the nuts and bolts took an age to loosen and he almost gave up, but in the end he triumphed. Lying in the sand under the vehicle wasn't comfortable but at least it was cooler than the sand in the sun. Hashim watched in awe and was continuously bringing water and wet towels; many of the soldiers also stood around and cheered Jeff on. That night, Jeff slept a good sleep.

The next shipment to the front was fast approaching and after that, the fleet would need to go to Cairo to replenish their stocks. Jeff had all the lorries working and off they set, fully loaded. He was proud of the fleet all lined up, travelling across the desert.

Jeff was in a lorry at the back of the convoy when there was a problem with a lorry, four from the front. Jeff jumped out and ran to the stricken vehicle. The driver said it started to splutter and was very jerky. Jeff was thinking that these soldiers could drive but their knowledge of their vehicle was close to zero.

He pulled the lorry out of line and told the convoy to carry on, he would catch them up. He was sure the problem was sand in the fuel line. He was opening the bonnet when Hashim started shouting and pointing towards the convoy. It was being attacked by Stukas. Jeff pulled the driver and Hashim under the lorry and hoped the German pilots wouldn't attack a broken-down vehicle. He was right, but the planes turned and attacked the back of the convoy and then flew back to their base. Jeff now had a problem.

"What shall we do?" asked Hashim.

"Fix this lorry and go and help the convoy. Flush the fuel line, while I check other potential problems."

Soon they were on their way and approached the convoy, where they were met by injured soldiers.

"The sergeant and driver of the front lorry are dead. Many of the injured ran to the back of the convoy and when the Stukas returned, they were sitting ducks."

"Get the good lorries moving and head to the front as fast as you can," responded Jeff. "Stay well apart.

Don't give them an easy target. Unload my lorry and put half the cargo on the left side of the road and the other half on the right. Make a barricade both front and back and set up two Bren guns. Who has used a Bren gun?"

Luckily, two soldiers had used one before. They were very happy to get behind their guns.

"Each of you will need a mate," Jeff continued. "If the Stukas come back, set up a crossfire and aim just in front of the propellers. Put all the injured in my lorry — I'll take them back to base and be back with some spares. Put the dead on the side of the road and if you have time, cover them with sand. Remember — we need to find them later."

The soldiers all responded, after all, this mate had been at Dunkirk. Jeff inspected the broken-down lorries and found the damage was to radiators and windscreens. The bullets had largely bounced off these old warhorses. He took a moment to stretch his hands out, they were not shaking. At Dunkirk, everything was shaking. He was in charge and maybe that had calmed his nerves. At the camp, he supervised the unloading of the injured and sent Hashim to collect spares. They were back on the road within twenty minutes.

Approaching the disabled vehicles, Jeff could see that the Stukas had been back. Several soldiers were excitedly waving and cheering.

One of the Bren gunners reported, "I think we hit two of their planes — there was smoke from two of them. The soldiers were under the lorries and we have no more casualties. I want to take this Bren gun everywhere I go."

The three lorries had no further damage. A couple of radiators and a few minor parts cured the problem. The only difficulty was that it was getting dark. Jeff had to make a decision, in the dark, if they tried to get to the front, they were liable to run off the road and get bogged down in the sand. On the other hand, the Stukas had noted their location and could come back after dark. He decided to drive a short way and separate the lorries, telling the soldiers to sleep under the vehicles.

Just before dawn, he had the three lorries moving and they made the front line. The captain who was in charge was very excited.

"Your soldiers may have shot down two Stukas!"

"I'm glad, sir. Just think of the headline — transport details are now shooting down enemy planes."

The return journey was uneventful. After reaching their base, they had to prepare to go to Cairo to pick up supplies and more men. Jeff had a list of spares he needed and now he knew where to go and what to say to get there. The quartermaster commander was in his office when Jeff knocked on his door. As he entered, he saw the Worcester major. They all saluted.

"I assume you are here for petty cash," the commander said. "I still have some from your last venture."

"Yes, sir. We were attacked by Stukas and my lorries are all still working but we need to keep them all right."

"I still have the small change since his last visit," the commander said, turning to the major. "But he is the cheapest supplier of parts in Cairo. I have traders in my office but the best comes from Birmingham."

"I have met this corporal before," the Worcester major replied. "And with an army of men like him, we would win any war."

Jeff was blushing now and realised his promotion was due to the major. Jeff received his Egyptian money and was about to leave, when the major said, "Can I come with you?"

"Yes, sir. But you must be well in the background."

Now both officers were laughing.

The parts market was very busy and as Jeff strolled through, he noticed a man following him. He wandered over to a lorry he had hired and as he approached, he whispered to Hashim he was being followed. He kept on walking. Hashim challenged the man and found the sellers wanted to know why Jeff wanted the parts.

"I have some broken-down old lorries that I'm fixing to sell," he told the follower. "It is my business and he just identifies the parts and then I buy. The 'Khawaja' has no interest in my company. He is a friend of my family."

Hashim received the list from Jeff and took the follower back to the sellers. This time, negotiations were more difficult and Hashim had to explain that the '*Khawaja*' was a friend of his father and was doing a favour; he did not receive backsheesh. Negotiations became tough, so Hashim said he would try to find the parts elsewhere, a contact in Alexandria said there were parts there. The sellers came to an agreeable price; slightly higher than last time, but still cheap.

Jeff was standing with the Worcester major and he witnessed all this with amusement. This was very un-army. Jeff had asked him to keep quiet but occasionally, he couldn't supress a sudden laugh.

After returning the change and the list of parts to the quartermaster, they returned to the camp to unload.

"You're not leaving tonight, so I want you come to dinner with me, both of you, You can call me Reggie but not in front of other soldiers. I know you are Jeff and Hashim, so no need for introductions. I'll pick you up later and Jeff — you should wear uniform. Hashim — you can wear anything that is clean."

"Jeff," said Hashim, "I must go home to get new clothes. I won't be long. My family do not live far and my mother will have clean clothes."

"You know, Reggie, I never thought of Hashim's home and now I want to meet his parents," mused Jeff, as Hashim departed. "They must be middle class as they sent their son to English school."

"Next time you come to Cairo, we can both go together to see them, if I'm still here."

The dinner was at one of the best hotels in Cairo. At the table, they met another major, a friend of Reggie's. He was from New Zealand. Hashim was almost speechless at the company and the magnificence of the hotel. He was able to get out a small speech.

"My father thanks you all for getting me under your arm."

"Hashim — it is 'under your wing', like the angels. And Jeff is your angel."

"Yes, sir. I'm a Copt and understand angels."

The New Zealand major started to quiz Jeff about his fleet and Jeff shot a glance at Reggie, more or less asking whether he was able to give out information.

"Jeff, Ralph is my friend and a senior allied officer. You can tell him everything."

"First, let me say I came from one problem to another and now I have settled better into my new problem. Dunkirk was completely out of my control but a fleet of lorries has me believing that I'm in control."

Jeff then described his ageing fleet, all the problems that could arise in the desert and the potential part failures. All the time, the desert sand was stressed as the problem. If a convoy was attacked, the radiators were the most fragile part and then there was the loss of water.

Ralph listened intently to the information Jeff was giving and then said, "We'll soon have a fleet of new vehicles, I hope, and I'm assuming we'll have many of the problems you describe. Back home, I have a large farm and our problem is clay soil and plenty of rain. I would say that at any given time, half our fleet is under repair. Actually, it's my father's farm but he will retire when and if I get home."

"*Inshallah,* you'll get home safely, sir."

"Thank you, Hashim, I'll be glad to take that hope with me."

At the end of the meal, Reggie organised a jeep for Jeff and Hashim and the two majors stayed for an extra drink or two.

"Thank you, Reggie, for inviting me to dinner," Ralph smiled. "I learnt more from Jeff than I've learnt from many lectures. As you know, we'll soon be on the road to push the Germans back and I wish we had those two with us. I'd love to see this fleet Jeff talks about."

"They will leave about dawn and you could see the equipment I would have scrapped directly after the First World War."

Ralph stood on the road and saluted, as Jeff drove by. Hashim waved back and then saluted. This fleet was running well. Jeff and Hashim made several trips to the front and to Cairo and on one trip, Jeff met Hashim's parents. Reggie had moved on but had sent his regards. Hashim had made many friends in the market and now he did not have to haggle over prices. He found that some of the 'newer' parts came from other markets.

Jeff was now a sergeant and in charge of the fleet. The war in the desert was going back and forth until Rommel appeared. Jeff told Hashim that this bloke was something special and you should never underestimate your enemy.

Jeff was very thankful that his convoy was never attacked. He was grateful to Rommel. Maybe the Stuka pilots thought that these aging lorries were not worth the bullets. Jeff was never able to contact Reggie or Ralph but he knew they were busy and hoped they were alive. Jeff often laughed to himself that his best friends were a young Egyptian and two majors. One day, towards the end of the war, Hashim asked whether they could keep some of the lorries. That set Jeff off to see the quartermaster commander.

"Could we write off a couple of lorries? They are getting too old and frail."

"Oh Jeff, you should be in my position. We would have made money on the war, instead of losing it."

The war had not ended but Hashim had two lorries, gratis. Jeff allowed him to go on leave and start his business. When peace was declared, Hashim went to the quartermaster commander to bid for the rest of the lorries. The commander smiled to himself.

"I'm sorry — at the moment, I have no instructions regarding what to do with surplus equipment. Shortly there may be more equipment available, I'll let you know. If you become President of Egypt in a few years, I'll not be surprised."

"Sorry, sir. I'm a Copt and there is no chance of that happening."

Jeff had orders to return to England to be demobbed. He was loath to leave Cairo but looking forward to England and seeing his family. He had a good farewell with Hashim, he was in tears as his teacher was leaving. He escorted Jeff to the dock and pleaded with him to come back to Cairo.

Jeff was standing at the dock and a familiar ship was going to be his transport. By coincidence, he boarded the same destroyer that had brought him to Egypt, and was reunited with his sailor friend. They told story after story and the voyage passed in a flash.

Part 2

Landing in England wasn't the delight Jeff had expected. He was sent to Aldershot to be demobbed and given travel vouchers to Birmingham. He looked at his group of demobees, some were very happy but a few looked not so happy. Jeff thought he fitted into the latter group. He was going home to a wife he had not seen for five years and a daughter who was only two when he left. What do you say to a daughter who has not seen you for five years?

Arriving home, he was greeted by a young girl who screeched in his ear and hugged him very tightly. His wife, Doreen, appeared but her greeting was less enthusiastic. Jeff was so happy to sleep in his own bed but Doreen kept her distance. He realised they were not the same people as before. Maybe Doreen was worried he was going to become a boss and take over the job she had during the war. He had no intention of taking over, so he had to be patient.

He quickly found a job in a bus garage and loved fixing those big brutes. His daughter, Julie, was all over him and he had to tell her stories about Egypt, but Doreen seemed uninterested. He was now in foreign territory and so, in the evening, he went to the pub for a couple of beers. Actually, he preferred the cold Egyptian beer. One evening, one of the patrons got drunk and started talking very loudly.

"Them Yanks, came with their money and enjoyed a good time with our women."

He was looking at Jeff and even though his mates pulled him to a corner, he was still looking at him. Jeff left the pub early and on his way home, he tried to work out his next move. He decided to talk to the mechanics in the bus garage. He found there were very many Americans billeted around Birmingham and dances at the Res (Reservoir) and some church halls were popular with the ladies.

Now he had a problem. He had a beautiful daughter he had to protect, but he had to find out the truth. One day, he left work early and went straight to Doreen's wardrobe. Under a shoe box, he found some letters. As he read the first one, his suspicions were confirmed. It was from an American sergeant, professing his love for Doreen and wanting to take her back to the States. He had to confront Doreen, but not in front of Julie. The opportunity came when the Girl Guides were camping over the weekend and although Julie was bit young, they wanted to take her. Jeff enthusiastically said yes and Doreen had no objections.

After Julie left, Jeff asked Doreen about an American who wanted to take her to the States. Doreen was quite calm as she said she wanted to be with him.

They sat and looked at each other. There was no flaming row.

"That's it, then," Jeff said. This was a sort of anti-climax.

That night, Jeff slept on the sofa and when Julie came home, he explained he had nightmares about the war and he decided not to wake everyone. He would sleep on the sofa. This charade worked for a few days and one day, Jeff arrived home to find no Doreen. Julie arrived from a neighbour and Jeff asked what she would like for dinner.

"Baked beans on toast."

"I think I can do that. Would you like pepper or salt on that?"

"No salt and a little pepper, but have the sauce handy."

Jeff looked at his daughter and thought — this little girl has given me an order. Doreen had not returned by the next morning and Jeff prepared egg on toast. Julie looked at Jeff.

"She's run off with that American."

Jeff was taken aback. His young daughter knew more than he did. He wanted to respond but all he could say was, "She will probably come back."

"No, dad. There is just the two of us."

As he sent Julie off to school, he had a problem. Who could he call for help? His parents were dead and his elder sister was in New Zealand. He really had no friends in the area, but there was Reggie in Worcester.

Did he dare to ask for help? He had only been demobbed a month and he had a problem. He wrote a letter asking for advice and a reply came back by return mail. Jeff and his daughter were invited to Worcester on the following Saturday morning. Reggie advised how to get to his house after arriving by bus to Worcester.

Julie was excited as they crossed the bridge over the Severn and was happy it was a sunny day. As they arrived at the house number, they were both astonished at the length of the drive. As they approached the house, Julie became excited. She had never seen such a large house. Reggie opened the door and grabbed Jeff, pulling him inside.

"This is not my normal greeting, but I'm so glad to see you. And you must be Julie."

"Yes, sir. I thought you were going to kidnap my dad."

"Little lady, you have upstaged me. Let me kiss your hand. Your father is my best friend and so we are allowed to hug."

Reggie then introduced his wife, Sophie, who shook hands with Jeff and moved to Julie. As they moved together, Julie said, "I think that ladies shaking hands is a bit awkward. Can I have a hug?"

"You certainly can. I haven't had a hug for a long time."

"Your daughter has just melted my wife," Reggie whispered.

"May I show your daughter our house?" Sophie asked.

"Of course. I want to talk to Reggie in private."

After the ladies had left the room, Reggie said that Sophie was normally quite reserved with strangers but not with Julie, this was something new. They chatted about their problems. Doreen's disappearance wasn't unusual and the war had produced many marital breakups. Reggie was hearing many bad stories, mainly involving the soldier kicking his wife out, or just leaving home. A wife leaving home was more unusual, especially when a child was involved. At this point, Sophie entered the room and said she hoped they would stay the night. Jeff said they had no change of clothes but Sophie said they would find clothes.

"My wife is not impulsive; your daughter has just changed her."

Reggie explained that as it was Saturday, they only had a light dinner and then they would go to the local pub. Sophie was emphatic that the men go to the pub and she would stay with Julie. This pub was nothing like Jeff's local, there were soft seats and an array of beers. There was carpet on the floor and the brass rail at the bar was polished. Reggie was greeted by several of the patrons and their English was like the announcers on the BBC. Jeff was a bit intimidated but Reggie said if these people knew of his war record, they would be queuing to get his autograph. Jeff smiled at that remark. He couldn't imagine people wanting him to write his name.

After only two beers, they went back to the house. They were greeted by an excited Sophie.

"After looking around the house, Julie said that this large house needs children. She must have been reading my mind. By the way, she is asleep at the moment."

"I'm sorry if Julie has offended you."

"On the contrary — she has made up my mind. We have to adopt a child."

Reggie explained that they had discussed this subject for a long time. He preferred a boy but it had to be a girl now that Julie had mesmerised Sophie. The next morning, they went to breakfast.

"This is a beautiful table but I would like to sit close to my dad. Do you mind if I move the chairs?" Julie asked.

"No, I'll sit next to my husband."

"The only problem is, that leaves a lot of empty table," said Reggie.

They all laughed and carried on eating.

"Did you make this breakfast, Auntie Sophie?"

"No, we have cook. She doesn't normally come at weekends, but I told her you were coming."

"Well, give her my compliments. The food was delicious. Normally we have cereal but on weekends, we have egg and bacon. But her eggs and bacon were better."

"Shall we go and take a look at the garden?" said Sophie.

"Yes, but is there another way out, besides the front and back door?" asked Julie.

"I'm sure we'll find one. Let's go and see."

Reggie said that was a military question, how to break out of a property in a different way. Jeff told Reggie that when Doreen left, Julie set out a list of duties and they lived by them and there were only a few problems. At that time, Jeff felt he shouldn't show too much authority but he was glad that Julie had set the direction and it was a good one.

They were sitting at the breakfast table when Sophie came in, laughing.

"I have left Julie in the garden. Jeff, you have a remarkable daughter. I think she has entered my brain. I took her to a room where we could get out into the garden. She said she liked the room and the curtains, but they were very heavy and blocked out too much light. I'm standing there, nodding in agreement. We go to the garden, which she loves, and then she tells me we should have a vegetable garden as food is rising in price. She knows, as she goes to the market with her dad. She also shows me the ideal spot. I was thinking of a plot three years ago and it was in the same place. I must get back — she'll probably have more good ideas."

"Jeff, I saw what you did in Egypt but you have been upstaged by your daughter," smiled Reggie. "I have been away a lot and Sophie copes very well and now a young lady comes into her life and throws her like a horse throws a jockey. I'm the man in our relationship but I'm going to sit back and watch. I have been superseded by a young lady."

"I have a problem. My daughter is growing and she will be leaving junior school to go to senior school. She is so bright and could get into any grammar school, but they're so far away."

They were now interrupted.

"We are going to Worcester market. I'm informed we could get some bargains," said Sophie.

Jeff and Reggie took a stroll around the considerable gardens. Reggie explained that, as the second son, he inherited the smaller property but his elder brother was the farmer. He was so grateful to Jeff for bringing his daughter into their lives. Sophie was becoming depressed that they couldn't have children. Julie had changed her in one weekend. His other news was that he was in touch with Hashim and Ralph. Apparently, Hashim was doing well with a fleet of lorries and thought of Jeff whenever he had to fix one. The quartermaster stayed in Egypt and they were now good friends. Maybe that was how he had found Reggie's address. Ralph sent his regards and said that if Jeff were passing, he had a couple of tractors to be fixed.

The ladies returned with lots of bags, mainly fruit and vegetables for the cook. After lunch, Julie met the cook and thanked her for a delicious meal. Sophie took Julie into a large drawing room and asked if she would like to do a jigsaw. Julie had never tried a jigsaw and when she got the hang of it, she was good at finding and fitting pieces. The jigsaw wasn't finished when it was time to leave and Sophie said they would leave it undisturbed until next weekend. Sophie then asked Jeff if they would come next weekend. Reggie could pick them up this time. Reggie apologised for not picking them up this weekend, but he had a meeting on Saturday morning.

"I hope we are not interfering with any of your plans?" said Jeff.

"Certainly not. You make our house alive, you make us alive. Our house is big, but Julie has a way of filling it."

As they entered the car, Julie said she couldn't invite them into her house as they had not tidied up before leaving. She would be ashamed of them seeing the mess.

Jeff breathed in deeply. Reggie smiled and Sophie said she understood. The drive into Birmingham seemed very short as Julie had a comment about almost every sight. They dropped Jeff and Julie at the end of their passageway, and then Reggie and Sophie set off, back to Worcester.

"That was the best weekend I have ever spent, apart from our honeymoon, of course. She told us what to do politely and then gave us the reason. Most adults would have shied away from the reason, but she is so open."

Reggie now opened the crucial subject. "How about adoption?"

"Yes. We are never going to get a Julie, but I want to adopt a small girl."

"After seeing Julie, I have no objection."

That evening, bedroom pleasure was one of the best.

The next weekend, Reggie pulled up at the entry to be greeted by Julie, calling her dad. "I'm sorry if I was rude last week by not inviting you into our house. You can see it when we come back."

Sophie moved into the back seat with a tear in her eye.

Reggie asked Julie if she had ever been to a farm and she had not.

"My brother has cows, pigs and chickens."

"Can you get fresh eggs and milk?" asked the little girl.

"Yes, but you have to kill the pigs to get the bacon."

"Uncle Reggie, you have made my day even before we get there."

This was the first time she had called him 'uncle' and the grin on his face lasted the whole trip. The farm was near Bridgenorth and as they entered through the gate, Julie had her first sight of a cow.

"Is that a cow or a bull?"

"The sack hanging below her hind quarters is called the udder and the teats are where you get the milk. Be careful when you're close, they can push you out of the way with a movement of their body."

The car stopped and as they climbed out, they were greeted by Ralph, Reggie's brother and Gwen, Ralph's wife. Julie went for the hug again and Gwen said to Sophie that she would love to have a daughter, she had two sons. Sophie replied that a daughter like Julie would be heaven. Sophie admitted she was in love with Julie, she had an ability to read her mind.

Julie was amazed at the size of the cows and weight of the fat pigs. She chased the chickens until Ralph said they might not lay so many eggs if they were tired. She apologised and hoped she had not spoilt their egg-laying. Ralph laughed behind his hand and said this girl could lighten any situation.

Lunch was plentiful and Julie complimented the cook.

"I'm the cook," Gwen said. "I love to cook and with two sons, I have to cook a lot."

"Then my compliments are doubled," said Julie. "I don't think I have ever eaten a better lunch."

Ralph turned to Jeff and Reggie. "This girl should be a diplomat."

The men retired to the pub for a couple of quick beers before closing time. In the discussions, it turned out that Ralph was having trouble with a couple of tractors. Jeff volunteered to help but he had no work clothes. Ralph had clothes and Reggie, Sophie and Julie could go to Worcester while Ralph would take Jeff to their house when he had finished.

Reggie, Sophie and Julie left and Jeff had new working clothes.

"One tractor has a clutch problem. I don't think it's the gear box. The other has a problem with the back axle and I would need a pit to examine them both. If the parts are available, they could be fixed, but a pit is a necessity."

"I have a friend with a garage and two or three pits. Could I pick you up after work on Friday and you and Julie could stay here, or at Reggie's?"

"I'll need some large tools but they're not available in most garages."

"My friend fixes some lorries so he might have heavy tools. How much do I owe you?"

"Nothing. You have treated us to a magnificent lunch and as you're Reggie's brother, I couldn't take a pound. When I have cured your problem, we can talk."

When Jeff returned to Worcester, there was great rejoicing, the jigsaw was finished. The three men went to the pub and Ralph learned of Jeff's war record, mainly from Reggie. Reggie also admitted he made friends with a New Zealand major because his name was Ralph. Ralph stated that after seeing Julie, his wife Gwen wanted a daughter.

The evening dinner was quite quiet and Julie said she was tired. Sophie said that in a few weeks' time, she would be going to a cottage they had near Woolacombe, in North Devon, and asked could she take Julie.

"Julie has never seen the sea or sand, so if I say no, I'll break her heart. Yes, of course — but she has no beach clothes."

"Don't worry about that. Next weekend, we'll go shopping on Saturday. Tomorrow being Sunday, most of the shops will be closed."

"My wife generally goes for two weeks," said Reggie, "and comes back after one week, as she's bored."

"That won't happen this time. Julie will keep me entertained for at least a month. Don't tell her until next week."

The next Friday, Ralph picked up Jeff and Julie and took them straight to the garage owner, who had stayed open late.

"Good evening, Mr Smith. My dad is an expert mechanic and we'll look around the garage to see if we have everything we need."

"Yes, madam."

Ralph was trying to keep a straight face and Jeff apologised for his daughter's comments.

"I have women telling me what to do all day and I always say yes, but I must admit she is the youngest."

The next day, Jeff was up bright and early and later, Sophie and Julie went shopping. Jeff looked at the back axle and found a worn bearing, which he removed, and sent Ralph to find a new one.

"Mr Smith, do you mind if I occupy another pit so I can look at this clutch?"

"No, we have little work this weekend. To tell you the truth, work has slowed down. There's not much money around," answered the garage owner.

Ralph had bought the correct clutch and it was fitted before he returned with the bearing. The bearing was fitted before lunch and both tractors were in the forecourt by noon. They were about to leave the garage when a farmer drove a very old lorry in. Jeff became emotional, this was the same lorry he dealt with in Egypt.

"Arnold, we're about to close," Mr Smith said.

Jeff butted in and asked what the problem was.

"Trouble starting," stated the driver, "and then she splutters and gasps."

"I know this kind of beast. I'll take a quick look at it."

Jeff thought there couldn't be sand in the petrol pipe but he cleaned it, anyway. Then he cleaned the spark plugs and set the cleaned points, the beast started first time and the farmer did a jig.

"Parts for this lorry may be hard to find, but when I have time, we should drive around some scrap yards," said Jeff, wiping his hands. "If I were in Egypt, I'd know where to go but there must be some parts in this area. Working on this beast was a pleasure and bought back many happy memories, let me tell you."

The farmer pulled out a wad of notes and peeled off twenty, which he proffered to Jeff.

"No, that's too much."

"No? Now I have to buy you a beer and if I see you in Worcester, there will be lots more beers. I keep this old beast because it was my father's, which he bought after the First World War, and it has served us well."

In the pub, Jeff related many stories of his time and of Hashim, who had a fleet of these beasts. Ralph declined the third beer as he had to drive Jeff to Reggie's place and then go home to an anxious wife. Jeff said he would drive one of the tractors to the farm on Sunday. Mr Smith said he had witnessed more completed work in one morning that would have happened in five days in his garage.

Jeff was tired when he reached Reggie's house, but he had to stay awake for a fashion show. Julie had two swimsuits, sandals, a large colourful towel and a bucket and spade. Jeff looked at Sophie and pulled out twenty pounds.

"Definitely not. I have just been entertained for a whole morning, it was my pleasure. We had shopkeepers saying to come back again. They never say that to me when I'm alone."

Jeff excused himself as he was a bit weary and wanted a lie down. Ralph related what had happened that morning, Jeff had worked relentlessly and when Arnold arrived, Jeff was almost dancing at the sight of the lorry. Tomorrow they would drive the tractors to the farm, if Reggie would drive them to the garage. Reggie laughed as he said the other Ralph in New Zealand had problems with tractors.

The next morning, they drove to Mr Smith's garage to be greeted by Arnold with a basket of fruit and vegetables.

"My wife tells me I'm a mean bugger and for once, I agree with her."

They drove the tractors back to the farm and Gwen laid on a splendid breakfast.

"How much do I owe you?" Ralph asked Jeff.

"You try those tractors for a week because with machinery you fix one problem and another appears" Jeff replied. "Your family has done so much for me, I can't take from you but I realise you may not be comfortable with that, so let's talk next week."

They drove home with twenty quid in Jeff's pocket, new clothes for Julie and a box of vegetables, a good weekend. In the week, Jeff spotted an advert in the newspaper, emigration to Australia for ten pounds per person. This seemed to be an omen.

Ralph picked them up on Friday afternoon and was very happy his tractors were both working. He wanted to take them to see Arnold and his wife. Jeff was okay with that as he wanted to see the lorry. Julie was surprised when she saw the lorry, as it was so old. Arnold and his wife had the girl's normal greeting and Arnold's wife was very pleased with a hug. The two sons were a little bit reserved, but they liked Julie.

"With four of you running this farm, I assume you have a schedule."

"What do you mean?"

"My father and I have a routine, he does some things and I do others, so everyone knows their responsibilities."

"We have no schedule but your routine is worth a try. Thank you for the idea."

Again, there was fresh fruit, vegetables, eggs and milk. Just after the war, these were highly valued items.

Sophie was so glad to see Julie, she had a new jigsaw puzzle. Ralph was telling Reggie that Jeff could make a living in this area, fixing broken farm machinery. Once word spread, he would have lots of work.

"Work is not Jeff's problem," explained Reggie. "He has a very bright daughter coming up to leaving school. We could have him in Worcester but he must make up his own mind. Work is not a problem; friends are not a problem, but blood relatives are a problem. He has a sister, Constance, in New Zealand. While Julie is in Devon, he will investigate going to Australia. He has some money saved after fixing your tractors and other farmers' machinery."

Ten pounds each to go to Australia, Jeff was even wondering if he might not have to pay for Julie. He discussed his proposal with Reggie and tried to see if he could arrange the voyage to have a week in Egypt. Reggie wasn't happy with their leaving but understood the motive. Since Jeff had come into their lives, he was much closer to Ralph, Jeff and Julie had a way of bringing people together. Reggie decided he must take Sophie to Egypt.

Reggie and Jeff drove to Devon and found an excited pair of females. Julie showed them her shell collection. Sophie said she had tasted barbecued fish, which was the best she had ever tasted. A man caught a fish and Julie asked whether he would eat it. The man said that we would all eat it and then he started a fire and cooked the fish. Julie asked when it would be done and he told her his wife would come when she smelled the fish was edible. Sure enough, his wife appeared, Julie gave her a hug and they all ate the most amazing fish.

"Julie has a way with people," Sophie concluded. "It's a combination of her innocence, inquisitiveness and the ability to ask interesting questions. I hope we can adopt a girl as good as her."

The swimsuits had all been used and Julie was learning to swim. Sand was very nice but it got everywhere. Jeff thought that very funny, he had battled sand for all his time in Egypt. Things were always 'sandified'.

Jeff explained they were going to Australia to be closer to Auntie Constance. They would see Uncle Hashim in Egypt. Sophie was very upset but realised Jeff was doing what he thought best. He had built up a group of friends in Worcester and they were all loath to see him go.

The day arrived. Reggie and Sophie took them to Southampton to catch their boat. Julie was excited she had never seen a bigger ship and Sophie was in tears as they said goodbye. Jeff hugged Reggie and Sophie.

"Come to Australia — but at least get to Egypt."

"I'm planning a trip to Egypt in the near future," Reggie responded, "but a visit to Australia will be in the far future. Give our regards to Hashim and tell him Sophie and I will try to see him in a few months."

The parting was sad for the adults but for Julie, it was a new adventure. Jeff was thinking about Egypt but after that was the big unknown. He had not seen his sister for many a year. Sophie gazed fondly at Julie.

"We can only see the past but she can see the future. This girl is going places."

Part 3

Jeff had arranged that they would leave the ship in Cairo and catch another boat in about ten days. Jeff and Julie had a small cabin, but at least it had a porthole. Their luggage was pretty minimal; two swimsuits were the first to be packed. Jeff had persuaded Julie that she would love Australia as there were so many beaches.

Julie's first observation was that this was a big ship, but there weren't many places to go. The next was that the sea was so big, as they spent a few days out of sight of land.

"Dad! Look at this mountain. We're going to dock here — can we get off?"

"No," Jeff shook his head." This is Gibraltar. We'll pick up some passengers but I don't think we'll be let off. I've passed here before and never set foot on land."

The ship sailed across the Mediterranean straight to Egypt. The next wonder was the Suez Canal, where Julie was fascinated by the waterway. She wanted to stay on the deck all day. They were to get off at Suez and be picked up by Hashim. Jeff was hoping Hashim would have something more comfortable than an old lorry.

As they disembarked, Jeff saw Hashim standing next to a four-door limousine with a big smile on his face. Jeff hugged Hashim and then introduced Julie. Hashim kissed the girl's hand. Julie looked around and she could see was sand.

"You're not the first man to kiss my hand," she laughed.

"May I not be the last. Welcome to my country — a place saved by your father. Jeff called me 'son' so you must be my sister."

Julie looked quizzically at Jeff.

"He is exaggerating. I was a small cog in a very big wheel. I was one soldier in a large British Army. Hashim was my right-hand man and as Brummies do, I called him 'son'. But if I had a son, he would be first choice. Now Hashim, have you borrowed this swanky car?"

"No, Jeff. I bought it at auction with the help of a friend; someone you know very well and who is hoping to see you."

The ride to Cairo was interrupted regularly by Julie saying, "Did you see that?"

Both Hashim and Jeff were smiling. Arriving at Hashim's parents' house, there was a reception committee. Jeff shook hands with everyone and Julie did her usual, shaking hands with the men and hugging the women. She had them all in the palm of her hand. Hashim introduced his wife Sarah, who was pregnant. They already had one son.

"Hashim, you're a fast worker. How's business?"

"I have four of our old beasts and two newer American trucks, as they call them. I have good drivers and we are carrying anything, but mainly fruit and vegetables. Believe it or not, the scrap yards are some of our biggest customers for fruit and vegetables. I'm teaching one of my cousins to be a mechanic, but sometimes I have to get my hands dirty."

"Dad come and see Nabil, Hashim's son. He's gorgeous," said an excited Julie. "Sarah says he likes me as he smiles all the time I'm near. I don't always understand everything that is said, but Sarah has good English."

"Hashim, my daughter says what she feels," smiled Jeff. "There is no barrier. I hope she doesn't upset your relatives."

"My wife is going to be so happy about her acceptable English. My mother has already whispered to me that this girl is going to be a star."

Ten days in Cairo passed in a flash. Jeff met the Quartermaster and they had a good lunch in a top hotel. The Quartermaster was the head of a large export-import company. He loved Cairo and decided to stay after the war. Julie spent a lot of time with Nabil, except for when she went to see the Pyramids and the Nile. When they left, there was a lot of ululating and wailing from the women. Julie promised to come back.

The voyage to Sydney was long and their first sight of Australia was Perth, where some people disembarked. Julie assumed they would be in Sydney the next day but stops in Adelaide and Melbourne soon removed that notion. Jeff had anticipated getting off at Sydney but he was told they were going to Brisbane. Julie loved the harbour bridge, but she was now anxious to leave the ship.

Disembarking at Brisbane, the Immigration Officer was astonished. "You have a job lined up, accommodation, and your daughter is enrolled in a local school. You must have a skill we really need."

Jeff thought this must be Reggie's work.

Jeff's job was in a bus garage and the accommodation, although a bit rough, was adequate. Julie's first day at school was a little difficult but once she mentioned Dunkirk and Egypt, two of the girls told her their fathers were in Egypt. Fewer girls called her a Pom and when she talked about Egypt, she made more friends. Within a week, Jeff had met two fathers who were in Egypt and one man who was at Dunkirk; Julie had been invited to a couple of parties.

After a few weeks, Jeff found a furnished flat to rent in St. Lucia, near the University of Queensland. The furniture was sparse but Julie liked the area and told Jeff they could slowly get more furniture. Jeff could get as much overtime as he wanted but he did not like to leave Julie alone. He contacted his sister, Constance, and she said she would visit them for two weeks. Julie was excited, as was Jeff, he had not seen his sister for many years. They met at the airport where Constance and Jeff hugged and kissed. Julie hugged her, saying, "You are my real aunt and I have not seen my father kiss another woman."

"But you have not kissed me yet."

"Don't worry," laughed Julie. "You'll get many kisses."

Jeff took them back to the flat and explained he would be back soon, but he had to fix a bus that needed to go out in the morning.

"Don't worry. Julie and I will have a chat."

When Jeff returned, he asked Julie to go into the garden as he wanted to talk to Constance.

"Your daughter is amazing," his sister declared. "She started by showing me her swimming costumes, a thing I would expect of an eleven-year-old. Then she asked me if I had any children. We had a long discussion about childless marriage. She had advised your friends to adopt a daughter. I can't believe I was discussing a childless marriage with a girl of eleven! Then she tells me you need a woman companion and can I help? Next, she asks me about the political system in New Zealand. I'm talking to a young girl who acts like a twenty-year-old."

"Since Doreen left, I have never tried to stop her saying what she feels and she seems to have a way with people, especially women. She has organised our daily living, and in some ways, she relieves me of many responsibilities. She is so bright, I don't want to stop her. My job is to provide for her and I know she'll outstrip me in the future."

"I would love you to come to New Zealand. My husband is looking forward to meeting you."

"I have to stay at least two years in Australia, I think, but we'll save some money and visit you."

The next two weeks were just a delight for Julie. Constance hired a car and they toured Brisbane and went to the beach. Shopping for food was a delight, as Auntie Constance cooked some good meals. Julie had many new clothes and Jeff was telling his sister to stop.

"I have never shopped for a young girl and I'm enjoying every minute. Julie has interested me in adopting but I think we're too old."

Constance left after two weeks, and Julie said she was sad but planning on a visit. Constance lived in Wellington and Julie studied all the maps of New Zealand she could find. Jeff did lots of overtime and in the school holidays, they visited Constance and Harold.

Part 4

"She starts asking Harold about the New Zealand government system," Constance said, "as she has to write an essay when she returns to school. Harold thought it was a dry subject until he moved into her world. She asked him about the class system and then about the Maoris. He was very impressed and he was rethinking young girls, but I told him this may be a special one. We have a very bright niece."

"I like Harold. I never really met him when I was young but you made a good choice," Jeff mused. "Now, Constance, I would like to visit my friend in Invercargill. What's the best way to get there?"

"The only way to go there is to take my car. Take the ferry and then head down the east side of South Island; it's about as far as you can go. You'll have to stay overnight somewhere, depending on the roads."

"Is it all right if I leave Julie with you?"

"Yes, of course! I want to take Julie to our cottage near Thames, where they have hot springs. Harold has some conference or other and it will be a good time to get out of Wellington."

Jeff set off south, while Julie and Constance set off north. Jeff had been in touch with Ralph and he had told

Jeff to stop at a place called Timaru; a small town with a pub and a hotel. Jeff was expecting good roads but some parts were not so smooth, so it was late afternoon before he reached Timaru. He checked into the hotel and then went for a beer.

"Another Brummie — I don't believe it! In Timaru!"

Jeff had ordered a beer and this was the reception from the landlord. The landlord's wife, Irene, came out with a big smile.

"We're from Handsworth," she said. "What are you doing here?"

"I'm going to Invercargill. By the way, I'm from Rotton Park."

"That is the end of the earth and Rotton Park is close. Do you have a reason?"

"I'm visiting someone I know, who owns a farm, and I'm looking to fix his tractors."

"If you were in here later, this place would be filled with farmers and all of them would want tractors or lorries fixed. What do you do at home?"

"Well, home at the moment is Brisbane and there I fix buses. I want to come to live in New Zealand."

"Please do, as soon as you can. I'll cook you bacon and eggs — sorry, no black pudding. Trust a mechanic to come from Birmingham." With that, the wife left to go back to the kitchen.

"How much do I owe you for the food?" Jeff asked the landlord.

"Nothing, but don't speak too loudly, some of our patrons aren't even keen to pay for the beer."

Reaching Ralph's farm, Jeff was impressed with the farmhouse and the other buildings. Ralph was very welcoming, presenting his wife, father and mother. Ralph's mother asked how Jeff knew her son. Jeff recounted how he had met him in a hotel in Cairo, where he told him about the problems with transport in Egypt. After being at Dunkirk, he realised how transport had to keep working. As soon as he mentioned Dunkirk, everything relaxed (it worked again).

"Ralph, one of your tractors is just out of tune but the other has gearbox problems. I think it's the wet, heavy soil wearing out the clutches. What we need is a pit. I'm working out my passage but when I'm finished, I'll come to New Zealand, but if you can find a garage with a good mechanic, please use him."

"Jeff — you are a special man," Ralph responded. "You're telling me you can't break a contract and instead of telling me to wait, you are telling me to find another mechanic."

"Our friend Reggie has helped me so much, and in the future, I'm sure you'll be of help. How could I betray you both?"

Back in Wellington, Julie was so excited with the hot baths that Jeff had to wait until she had gone to bed to tell of his trip. Harold had never been south of Dunedin and wondered about Jeff's reception in a very conservative area. Jeff said Dunkirk squashed any reservations. He related that he met a couple of Brummies in Timaru and found out that many farmers had problems with transport. The South Island needed a lot of specialist help and Jeff thought there was a good living to be had there.

Returning to Australia, Julie was a bit upset but Jeff explained that he had to fulfil his contract, as how could you trust a man who broke contracts? Julie was writing and put that point into her essay. She received top marks for her essay and was called into the headmaster's office.

"Where did you get all this information?" he said.

"My uncle works for the New Zealand government and he told me a lot. But the essay is all mine."

"I'm from New Zealand and loved what you have written; I'll take it home for my wife to read. I really liked the line about not breaking contracts."

"Oh, that was my father's," replied Julie, proudly.

"You have a formidable family, you should go far."

The school year passed quickly and Julie was top of the class. Jeff approached the New Zealand office in Brisbane and found, as he had a skill they needed and with a sister in Wellington, that his passage to NZ would be smooth. Julie was already enrolled in the best girls' school in Wellington and when her headmaster found out, he was very impressed. Jeff had a good send-off, as he was well-liked in the bus garage.

Part 5

Arriving in Wellington, it was the school holidays, so Julie and Constance wanted to go to Thames. Jeff thought it was a good way to see the North Island. The cottage was like a large house and Jeff enjoyed the hot baths. He was able to talk to some local mechanics and found the proximity of Auckland was important in getting parts. Most of the big vehicles were sent there for repair or servicing. That settled his thinking, it was the South Island for him.

Travelling down the South Island, Jeff stopped at Timaru and entering the pub, he asked for bacon and eggs with black pudding.

"No black pudding for you. You're not in Smerrick now." Irene came rushing from the kitchen and hugged Jeff like a long-lost friend. Jeff explained he was on his way south but wouldn't mind talking to a few farmers.

"Don't drink too much. These men come from the fields with a thirst and it can get a bit hectic."

Jeff sat at the bar and drank slowly. He then started to meet some of the farmers. Machinery was always a problem and getting it fixed was a bigger problem. One man asked what Jeff was doing in the area. Jeff explained he was going to fix large vehicles, probably well south of Timaru. Another man asked his experience and as soon as he mentioned Egypt and Dunkirk, the bar fell silent.

"I have never seen this bar so quiet except when we're closed," marvelled Irene. "They're hanging on your every word."

"I know Dunkirk is a magic word and now I know Egypt has the same effect."

Jeff tried to explain that war was to be avoided, if possible, but many of the young men around wanted to join the army when they knew the location of the next war.

Irene explained that they were brought up with a rifle and often went hunting 'pugs' (pigs to us). The evening was very jolly and one man went home to bring back his father, who had been in Egypt.

Arriving at Ralph's farm, Jeff met an excited farmer.

"My dad died in Egypt and I promised my mother that any man who served in Egypt, I would help."

Jeff related his experience in Egypt and that his only contact with New Zealanders was with Ralph. The man left in tears. Ralph told Jeff that was the local bank manager.

"I thought he was a farmer, now he's a bank manager."

"He is both. Nearly everyone in this area does some farming and he has a large farm with a manager. By the way, I found you some transport, it's a motorcycle."

"I've never ridden a motorcycle."

"This one has a sidecar, where you can put your tools or friends."

"Very funny. But I always wanted to ride a motorcycle."

"Tomorrow," continued Ralph, "we'll go to look at this garage. It's been on sale for a while and I think we can try and rent it. After that, you can return your sister's car. If you get the ferry the next day, you can catch a bus to Timaru. I'll meet you there as I'm interested to meet your new friends."

"I'm taking up a lot of your time," said Jeff.

"Firstly, I'm your friend. Secondly, my father says you could be of great help to this area. And thirdly, the bank manager wants you to meet his mother."

They both laughed and set out to see the garage. Jeff wasn't expecting much but this was a well-laid-out garage with two pits. Talking to the owner, he found that the mechanic who ran the place was from the North Island and became homesick. They negotiated and Jeff took out a six-month lease with Ralph acting as surety. Jeff drove back to Wellington. The next day, he caught the ferry and then the bus to Timaru (a long ride). Jeff and Ralph met at the hotel and went to the pub.

Jeff shouted, "Two black puddings, no bacon and eggs!"

"You're pulling my leg, you bugger!"

Irene rushed out of the kitchen and gave Jeff a big hug and then she noticed Ralph and gave him a big hug, too. The landlord came over and shook their hands and a young patron came over and shook Jeff's hand.

"Who's your mate?"

"He is Major Ralph."

The man rushed out of the door as though he had been shot. Within ten minutes, the bar was crowded, several of the patrons knew Ralph. Jeff and Ralph had beers lined up at the bar. This was a raucous night and Jeff had too much to drink, as had Ralph. The drive back to Invercargill was full of the previous night and Ralph said that Australians seemed to be interested in where you were from, but New Zealanders were more interested in where you had been.

The next few weeks saw the business grow, as word spread through the district. Jeff found an owner with a low-loader and large machinery was coming in every day. He was in a local pub, one day, when a man approached him with a proposal.

"I have a son who wants to be a mechanic. This is a difficult area for employment. Would you take him on as an apprentice?"

"You have your timing right I was thinking of taking a young man to help me."

"We are Maoris."

"That doesn't matter to me. If he can do the job he is welcome, but if he is not suited then we'll part."

Nikau was sixteen and as soon as Jeff saw him, he knew he was going to be an ideal apprentice. He was physically strong and was very attentive to everything

Jeff said. Jeff let him help on some of the difficult jobs and when Jeff became tired, he let Nikau take over. If a difficult nut was loosened, Nikau let out a cry and Jeff called it a 'nut cry'.

One weekend, Jeff went to Wellington and left Nikau in charge. On his return, he found two difficult jobs completed. That night, in the pub, Nikau's father said his son had worked until nine p.m. and the next morning (a Sunday), he had worked until noon.

"I should pay him overtime," Jeff said.

"No — he didn't do it for money but for experience and you are giving him the best experience."

Jeff and Nikau worked well and as their reputation spread, the work was never ending. One day, a man who said he was an inspector from the government employment unit came to talk to Jeff about Nikau. Was he being treated correctly and was he being paid at the correct rate? Jeff called in Nikau, and asked if he enjoyed his work, and was he being treated fairly and paid fairly? Nikau decided to talk for several minutes and it was all praise for Jeff. When the man left, Jeff and Nikau had a good laugh.

Jeff had a small flat in Dunedin but wanted to invite Constance, Julie and Harold (if he would come) to visit. He asked Ralph if they could stay at his place. Ralph was very happy and said he would organise a dance. This was an old tradition and they had not done it for several years.

Constance, Julie and Harold met Jeff in Timaru. The group moved to the pub where Irene met Julie.

"A Brummie lass in our pub! This is a first."

"Actually, you have two, my aunt is from Birmingham," laughed Julie.

"I'm sorry, madam, the way you spoke, I thought you were a local."

"I've been here a long time," Constance smiled.

Soon the bar filled with locals when the word spread that Jeff was in town. Once they realised Harold worked for the government, the complaints came thick and fast. When Jeff explained that Harold was the sergeant major and it was the officers who made the decisions, things calmed down. Later, Harold told Jeff that he had never thought of himself as a sergeant major.

The next day they visited the garage, and Julie met Nikau. He explained he was covered in oil and grease so he couldn't shake hands. Julie said she understood as she had seen her father in a bigger mess. Jeff looked at Nikau and said, "Carry on working, son. You'll see her again."

Arriving at Ralph's house, there was a reception committee. Julie did her norm and the women were immediately onside. Harold met the bank manager and his mother and there was a connection. Constance was introduced to Ralph's wife, Angela, and there was a special bond. They had each met their husbands in England at dances for servicemen. Constance had met Harold in Birmingham, he was attached to an intelligence unit. Angela met Ralph in London, while he was on training in England.

Jeff went out to the paddock with Ralph and thanked him for the welcome. Ralph was so happy they were going to have a hooley, as they had not had one for many years. Many of the South Islanders were related to Scottish and Irish immigrants and it was a tradition to have a hooley once a year. The tradition had lapsed a bit recently, but Ralph was going to reintroduce it.

The next evening, they had the hooley. Jeff had asked if Nikau and his father could attend.

"Jeff, you are a very special man. I don't think any Maoris have ever attended such an event and I ask myself why. I have seen Nikau work and you have picked out a diamond. They are both very welcome."

Nikau and his father, Nikora, arrived to be greeted by Jeff and Ralph. Nikora admitted that he did not want to come but Nikau had forced him. Julie came over and shook hands with Nikau and his father and then left to join a group of women.

"My son is entranced," Nikora whispered to Jeff. They were joined by Harold and Constance, and Ralph whisked Jeff off to meet a lady.

Gladys was a widow. Her husband had fallen in France, she had a daughter and managed a smallholding. Jeff found this lady was easy to talk to and their stories often crossed in a good way. Jeff called Julie to meet Gladys and they hugged, then Julie took over. She basically told Jeff's life story.

When Julie left, Gladys said, "Can you add anything to your life story?" They both had a good laugh. Julie went to Constance and said she had found the woman for her father. Constance was still shaking her head when she met the bank manager. He told her that her brother was a man the area needed. It was so far south that people thought of it as somewhere else, she and her husband could change opinions. This was the first time Constance had been seen as a political animal.

Jeff and Gladys spent the rest of the evening together and Julie watched from afar.

"Come over tomorrow and meet my daughter. She is very shy."

"I'll bring my daughter, she's the opposite of shy. I call it un-shy."

The next day, Jeff and Julie visited Gladys and her daughter, Margaret. Julie took Margaret aside and said how well Jeff and Gladys were suited. Margaret was taken a bit off-guard, but said she would have to get to know Jeff before she could come to any conclusion.

"I understand. You'll like my dad, but might need time. I saw their compatibility at once."

Lunch was a success and Julie complimented Gladys on her cooking. The girls went off to the garden to feed the chooks (chickens).

"I wish my daughter was more like yours, she can dominate any conversation," sighed Gladys.

"She is very outspoken," Jeff responded. "But I never try to challenge her, I think — because she has no mother — she is the female adult. A few days with my daughter will change your daughter."

After two days, Constance, Harold and Julie were planning to return home.

"Margaret has asked me whether she could go to Wellington with Julie," Gladys enquired. "She has never been north of Dunedin. Last week she wouldn't say boo to a goose. I've talked to Constance and she says she will take care of her."

"I told you my daughter would change Margaret."

Margaret spent a week in Wellington. Constance and Julie brought her back to Timaru, where they met up with Gladys and Jeff. Irene served them.

"This Brummie keeps bringing new people to my pub," she said, "and I'm still trying to find black pudding."

They all laughed and later, Gladys asked, "What is black pudding?"

Margaret was a changed girl. She talked all the way home about Wellington and that she had been to so many places, including the Parliament building. Gladys was astonished, this was a new daughter. Margaret was talking about going to university and wanting to see Egypt and England.

Part 6

A few years passed and Julie was taking her final exams. She used her experience in Egypt in an essay, for which she received the highest marks. She had automatic entrance to any university and she picked Canterbury, in Christchurch. Jeff and Gladys were living together and Margaret had her sights on going to the same university.

Nikau was going out to farms to assess whether they could fix broken machinery. At first, some of the farmers only wanted Jeff to visit their farms but they soon realised that Nikau could do the job. Nikora would meet Jeff in the pub and was so pleased his son was learning a trade. He could set him up on his own one day.

"I want to send your son to Egypt. I have a friend who runs a fleet of lorries and I think it would be good for him to see different work conditions."

"Egypt! Have you talked about this to Nikau?"

"No. I have talked about my experiences in Egypt and he has said he would love to travel."

"Jeff, you have presented me with a problem. I'll discuss it with my wife and I'll get back to you. You are an extraordinary man. You have presented me with a dilemma I could never have envisaged."

Reluctantly, his parents decided to let Nikau go.

"Nikau, you'll be on this ship for many weeks," his father stated. "Keep a diary and see as much as you can. Your mother and I will expect many letters. In Cairo, you'll be representing our culture and you'll be representing Jeff. Do not do anything wrong."

Jeff had a new problem, how to replace Nikau. So he approached Nikora and asked if he knew of a suitable replacement.

"I have a nephew who lives north of Dunedin. He has a job delivering groceries but I'm sure he would love to be a mechanic. I can't guarantee he will be as good as Nikau."

Kai arrived and within one week took to the job. He was well-built, like Nikau, but not quite as smart. He was living with Nikora, rather like a replacement in Nikau's absence. Jeff had more work than he could do, he was thinking of expanding, but Gladys told him she would do the books. She would assess whether buying another garage was viable. Gladys had moved in with Jeff and had rented her property out.

Julie was entering her second year and Margaret was just entering her first year at university. Jeff and Gladys were enjoying their union and loving the success of their daughters. The girls were both at Canterbury University and sharing a flat in Christchurch. Margaret was no longer shy and was proving to be as smart as Julie. They had a good social life but they were both conscientious students. At holiday times, they would make their way to Timaru where Irene would give them a big welcome. Jeff and Gladys would pick them up and drive them back to a very overcrowded flat. Ralph always offered alternative accommodation and loved having the girls to stay for a while.

Nikau had arrived in Cairo and was working for and living with Hashim. Nikora was getting regular letters and was almost jealous of his son. Although the heat had affected Nikau at first, he was now enjoying the work. He was fascinated with Cairo. He had seen the Sphinx, the Pyramids and the museum. Hashim was going to take him to see the Suez Canal, this time from the land; he had previously seen it from the ship. One highlight was going to a huge hotel for lunch with some big-wigs, who were interested in his story.

Jeff had heard about Doreen through Constance. She had returned from America and wanted to contact Jeff. Jeff wasn't interested but thought he should tell Julie. She, too, was uninterested in seeing her mother but she told her dad that she was intending to take a year off and visit Egypt and England. Jeff decided against trying to dissuade her. The big surprise was that Margaret wanted to do the same. Jeff thought he should let Margaret tell her mother, so he contacted Margaret and asked what she wanted to do. This was the first time he had gone behind Gladys, but he thought Margaret was the one to tell her mother.

Finally, to Jeff's relief, Margaret told her mother and Gladys agreed, telling her to visit her father's grave. Jeff was surprised, there was no discussion or argument. Gladys explained that Margaret was now a young woman who was better educated than her mother, she would never win an argument.

Julie had set everything up. They would visit Hashim for a few weeks and then travel to England to stay with Reggie and Sophie. The girls would find part-time jobs in Worcester, then try to see a bit of England. Julie had all the ship time-tables, they would sail from Auckland with Constance's help. Margaret was so excited; her mother thought she had a new grown-up daughter.

Jeff started to tell Gladys about Birmingham and Worcester.

"Julie told you my life story when we first met, but there is a lot she doesn't know. I was born in Ladywood — a very industrial area. At the bottom of our street there was a canal and a railway line. Two streets away, the factories started and the smoke and smell of metal is still with me. When I was young there were very few cars, so we played in the street. Our houses were built in Victorian times but each house had an outside toilet. The houses were what we called 'two-up, two-down' homes with a living room, front room and kitchen on the ground floor and two bedrooms upstairs. As we grew up, and having an elder sister, I had to sleep in the front room. I suppose I was a bit jealous of Constance. Many houses in the area had communal toilets and washrooms, so we were better off than most people. Leaving school just before I turned fifteen, I was lucky to get a job in a garage, fixing cars and lorries. There weren't many private cars and I concentrated on lorries. I've told you about Dunkirk and Egypt, but not much about my homecoming. One thing that gets me about Dunkirk is that we were lucky to get away quickly. I was sent to Egypt without leave and later, when others were returning from Dunkirk, they were treated as heroes. Still, in many ways, being in Egypt shielded me from going back to France.

"When Doreen left, I was scared I would lose Julie and that would have been the end of me. As young as she was, Julie took over, she organised our lives. I was lucky that I had Reggie as a friend and of course, Julie captivated his wife, Sophie. We spent many weekends with them and they found me what we call 'foreigners' cash work at the weekend.

"Worcester is a rural town on the River Severn and there are many farms with lots of farm machinery that would break down, so my work with heavy machinery was in demand. Sophie loved having Julie around and Reggie's brother was a farmer with problem vehicles. He helped me get a garage to do my work at the weekends. I was tempted to move to Worcester but my only sister was in New Zealand. Through Reggie, I was lucky to meet Major Ralph and that's why we ended up in New Zealand, after a stint in Australia."

Gladys listened patiently. She had heard much of it before but she realised Jeff might be thinking he would lose Julie.

"She'll be back. She must come back as her love for her dad is so strong."

"At least she has to bring Margaret back," Jeff commented.

"Don't start me having second thoughts saying yes to her going."

Jeff met Nikora for their weekly drink.

"Nikau's recent letter upset my wife," Nikora confided.

"Why?"

"First, he said he's going to stay a little longer than planned. He had been out in the desert with the lorries to get an idea of the problems they encountered. Then he said he was learning Arabic, all good. He visited the war graves in Cairo and found a New Zealand section. There were two Maoris buried there and that made him very emotional. He could only say a few words in our language; he couldn't wish them well in heaven. He admitted he cried and said he would learn our language when he came home. When my wife read that, she started to cry and wouldn't be consoled. She is now teaching Kai our language. She's better at it than me."

"He might be there when Julie and Margaret visit," said Jeff. "That will be good for the three of them."

Nikau was in Cairo when the girls arrived, they had a few beers to celebrate. Hashim was so glad to see the girls and introduced Julie and Margaret to the family. Nabil (Hashim's son) was entranced by the girls. Hashim now had a compound housing his extended family, including his two small children. Margaret was drawn to these babies, whereas Julie wanted to interact with the older women. Nikau confided in the girls that he was in love with one of Hashim's nieces. The girls met Anna and talked to her. Her English was pretty good and although shy, she admitted that Nikau was good-looking. They thought her very attractive. Nikau took them to see the war graves and they were all emotional.

When the girls were leaving, Hashim gathered the family and talked about Jeff, he was the centre of everything. Hashim explained that there were two circles. He was in the first with Reggie and Ralph, and in the second were Julie, Margaret and Nikau. Jeff had made him rich and he had two friends at opposite ends of the world. Now his daughters and his student had graced his house, they would always be welcome.

Julie thanked Hashim and said, as her father had called him 'son,' he must be her elder brother. That brought clapping from the crowd and broad smiles from Hashim and his wife. Hashim wrote to Jeff that he wasn't happy to let them go. Nikau was such a good worker that if he wanted to come back to Cairo, he would make him manager of a new workshop he was building. The girls were so intelligent and mixed so well with his family, he was going to encourage all the young boys and girls to go to university.

Jeff couldn't wait for Nikau to come back, as he had plans to expand. If Nikau wanted to go back to Egypt, he wouldn't stand in his way. Kai was doing a very good job but Jeff felt he couldn't handle being in charge. Jeff had viewed a property north of Dunedin, not too far to attract business from the Timaru area. Gladys was more cautious and urged Jeff to wait until Nikau returned.

The girls arrived in England and went straight to Worcester. Sophie was most welcoming and introduced the girls to Tania, her adopted daughter. Reggie wrote to Jeff to say the women had taken over his house. Tania was in awe of the girls and Sophie was enjoying having young ladies about the house. The girls had visited Ralph; Margaret now had a part-time job on the farm and Julie had a job in a pub in the town. Her knowledge and experiences had brought in new custom and the landlord was very happy.

Nikau had returned and was working well with Kai, allowing Jeff to visit the farming areas and assess possible business. Nikau was learning his language and confided in Jeff that he wanted to go back to Egypt, he planned to get married. Jeff asked whether Nikau could live in Egypt and whether he had told his parents his plans. Nikau said he was working on it and Jeff said he should do so soon. Kai was learning a lot from Nikau and was fascinated with stories about Egypt.

Jeff realised that if Nikau left, he would have to find a senior mechanic, even if he did not buy another garage. Gladys helped him advertise the position and later helped him interview the candidates; she had become a very important part of the business. They had moved to a three-bedroom house and were enjoying their partnership. Two candidates stood out and Jeff persuaded Gladys they could buy another garage and employ both men. Jeff was looking at his life and marvelling at how a poor Brummie lad was doing so well.

Meanwhile, in England, Julie and Margaret had travelled to France to see Margaret's father's grave. Margaret never knew him as she was a toddler when he left for Europe. Nevertheless, it was an emotional experience for both girls. They were both astounded at the number of graves.

They had been to Birmingham a few times but Julie said that there was something she should do alone. Constance had given Julie Doreen's address and Julie had decided there was something she must do. She found the address and knocked on the door. Doreen answered and tried to hug Julie but she backed away.

"I came to wish you goodbye. That is more than you did to me and my dad."

"I'm your mother," Doreen stated.

"I have two mothers, Aunty Constance and Gladys, my father's partner, and I don't need a third. Goodbye."

With that, Julie walked swiftly away, ignoring her mother's pleadings. Doreen was left crying.

Reggie and Sophie took the girls to Southampton to catch their ship. All the ladies were in tears, but Margaret said she might come back. She was going to finish her degree and then hoped to renew her friendship with a local chap. On the way home, Reggie said to Sophie he wasn't sure which of Ralph's sons had taken her fancy.

Southampton to Auckland was a long journey with plenty of time to chat. Inevitably, the discussion moved to their parents.

"I loved your mother from the first I saw her, she is so right for my dad," declared Julie. "I hate my real mother — she left without saying goodbye to me. I understand how I must have been in the way, with her having a boyfriend, but not saying goodbye to me was unforgivable. The one good thing about her leaving was that I did not have to share my dad. I never heard him say a bad word about Doreen, although he must have felt bad. He never raises his voice or gets angry. Although I have done some stupid things, he has never scolded me. Coming to England meant I could see my mother as I had her address. That day I went to Birmingham on my own, I went to see her. I had heard that her American love affair had fallen through but I needed to tell her goodbye. I never want to see her again and I don't expect I will."

"That first day you came to our house and told me your dad and my mother were suited to each other, I was in shock," Margaret responded. "I was very shy because it was just me and my mother. I then saw Constance and Harold, and Ralph and Angela, and decided my mother needed a man. I love your dad and you now have to share him with me and my mom. I think we can share anything — except maybe boyfriends, but as neither of us has one, there is no problem. What did your mother say?"

"I didn't listen. I just told her I had enough mothers and did not need any more."

"I find that sad, but I suppose I understand."

Jeff and Gladys had driven to Wellington, this time avoiding Timaru. They were staying with Constance and Harold, awaiting the arrival of the girls in Auckland. Gladys had never been to Wellington and Jeff had barely seen the town. They now saw Parliament House, a few fledgling wineries and several pubs. Wellington was very hilly and Jeff and Gladys enjoyed several walks. One evening, Constance produced old photos of young Jeff and their parents and grandparents. Jeff went quiet and Gladys noticed the change.

"What was the problem with those photos?" she asked, later.

"No problem with the photos, I was glad to see them. I used to have many of those photos but when I came back from the war, I didn't notice they were missing. When we went to Australia, I only had a few photos of Julie with Doreen or myself. I thought nothing of it and now I'm upset that I never showed Julie photos of her grandparents. I don't get angry very often, I have trained myself to control anger as it has no use. I'm angry with myself for not missing the photos and with Doreen for throwing them out."

"Yes, photos are very important. I have lots of my husband and Margaret has seen them. She was too young when he left for the war but he was her father. It is possible Constance has shown them to Julie."

"I hope she has, but that makes me sad as I should have been the one to show her. I feel a sense of failure."

"We should ask Constance."

"Julie has seen a few photos but you know Julie — she is a whirlwind moving on very quickly. She has never seen the whole collection."

Gladys confided in Constance that Jeff was really upset that Doreen must have thrown out the photos. When the girls arrived, they could look at all the photos with Jeff giving the commentary. When they returned home, she would give a commentary of her photos.

"That's a brilliant idea. When you're away from home, photos are so important. I want to see them again and see them through Jeff's eyes."

The girls arrived in Auckland to much rejoicing. They were full of stories but Julie said nothing about Doreen. The evening of viewing old photos was a great success and Jeff enjoyed answering lots of questions. Harold said it was a pity his family took very few photos. Julie said that they had some and asked if they would like to see them. Everyone was happy with photo viewing. Gladys and Constance started to notice something that bypassed Jeff and Harold. There were lots of photos of the girls with Ralph's sons. After the photo show, Constance and Gladys conferred and they both came to the same conclusion that something had happened, but what?

Arriving back in Dunedin, Gladys put on a photo show and Jeff could see her husband, she had never shown photos of him. Margaret had not seen the photos for a long time and she was excited. Julie's response was that they all knew each other through the medium of the camera. As they lay in bed, Gladys was saying that still photos were not sufficient, what was needed were moving pictures, like in the cinema.

"Did you notice something in the photos of the girls with Ralph's sons?"

"No, not really."

"Well, I'm not sure who is involved with whom, but there's something going on."

"Let them tell us in their own time. They are going back to university and they will probably change."

"Yes, but a woman wants to know."

Part 7

Nikau had gone back to Cairo and was now managing one of Hashim's workshops. Jeff felt that Kai was getting restless. At one of their pub meetings, Jeff asked Nikora whether he should send Kai to Cairo.

"Jeff, you are a different human being," Nikora exclaimed. "You seem to be looking out for everyone and ask permission when others wouldn't. Of course — I'll talk to Kai's family and my wife. She is in control but don't tell her."

The answer from everyone was positive and Hashim would be very pleased. When Jeff presented Kai with the ticket, he thought Kai's hug would crush him. Kai was sent to Wellington to get a passport and stayed with Constance and Harold. They made him so welcome. He wrote to his aunt that he had met a Maori politician and told him about South Island. He had seen the Parliament and all the boats in the harbour. The ship he was going to board was the biggest thing he had ever seen.

In Egypt, Nikau was enjoying life. He was infatuated with Anna and had realised Julie wasn't for him. He had to ask Anna's father whether he could take her out. Permission was granted but there had to be a chaperone, he relayed in a letter to his parents. His mother read the letter and sat back with a satisfied grin on her face.

"He has taken tradition back fifty or a hundred years, he is asking permission," she said. "Anna's parents must be good people to be protecting their daughter. I want to meet them."

"Jeff, you've presented me with a new problem," said Nikora. We have to go to Cairo. Kai has written that he and Nikau went to the cemetery and said lots of words to the departed. Now my wife has to see the cemetery. I think she wants to see it more than Anna. My feeling is that Nikau wants to marry Anna."

"Do you need money? I'll pay your passage," Jeff answered.

"No, but I might need a loan when we come back."

In Cairo, everyone was awaiting the arrival of Nikau's mother and father, Nikora and Aroha. They were met by a large, four-door car, driven by Nikau.

"Whose car is this?" Aroha asked.

"This belongs to Uncle Hashim. My car is too small for this journey."

"I'll sit in the front with my son and Kai can sit with his uncle in the back," said Ahora.

Kai put his hand on his uncle's arm. "This is not New Zealand."

Nikora saw a new Kai, Egypt had changed him.

Kai did a lot of talking in the back of the car. He had eaten in the most beautiful hotels and ridden around the pyramids on horseback. He wanted horses back in New Zealand. The conversation in the front of the car was more serious and Nikora had a lot of sympathy for his son.

"Do you want to stay in Egypt? It is not your country," said Ahora.

"I'll not stay here forever, but I have a boss I respect and Jeff is a boss I respect and love. Mom — this is different from New Zealand. I see something new every day and the people are so hospitable. Hashim and his family are so good — I'm welcome anywhere. I never felt that before. You have to meet Anna. Be careful — she's worried about meeting you."

Entering Hashim's compound, there was a crowd but they stood back as Anna approached Nikora. She kissed his hand and he was visibly shaken. She turned to Nikau and said, "I'm not sure how to greet your mother."

"Give her a hug. It works for Julie."

Anna gave Nikau's mother a hug and Aroha burst into tears.

"I hope I have not offended your mother."

Nikora interjected and said his wife was tired from the journey. Later that night, he asked his wife what the problem was.

"First, I thought she was too beautiful and then wondered was my son good enough for her. I have never had these thoughts before and I was confused. The only thing I could do was cry."

"Well, I'm not marrying her but I wouldn't say no. Nikau has a great life here. What I have seen so far is that it's not for us, but it suits him. Kai can't get enough of Egypt."

The next day they met Anna's parents and Hashim lightened the mood by bringing along a band. Kai was singing with the band, in Arabic. Aroha told Nikau, they had missed Kai's vocation, he was a singer. Kai told his aunt that with his English and a bit of Arabic, he was in demand but being a mechanic was why he was in Egypt.

Nikau took his father aside and told him he wanted to marry Anna and a wedding could take place while they were in Cairo.

"Let's tell your mother together, then if there is any argument, there are two of us," Nikora smiled.

Aroha listened intently to Nikau, who gave a long speech. When he was finished, she said he must come back to New Zealand to have another wedding. Both Nikau and Nikora were shocked and they all rejoiced with a hug.

Aroha started to go around the compound to visit the families. There were lots of small babies and she was enjoying herself. Kai took Nikora to the workshops and introduced him to the mechanics. Most of the introductions were in Arabic and Nikora was astonished at Kai's language skills. Kai told his uncle that although he had not been in Cairo long, he decided the only way to get on was to learn Arabic as quickly as possible. He boasted that his Arabic was better than Nikau's.

That night Aroha told Nikora how she loved the way these people lived. All the families helped each other and that was how their people used to live. Nikora told her about Kai's language skills. Maybe giving lessons in their language had inspired him. Tomorrow they were getting up early, as they were going to see the pyramids.

Everything was being prepared for the wedding and Aroha was very excited. Kai warned that the wedding ceremony could be very long and of course, Nikau would have to pay the dowry.

"Must he pay a dowry?"

"Yes, uncle. Do not worry — he has plenty of money. As best man, I have to give a speech and I intend to do half in Arabic. Your speech will be in English, so make it short."

"You are saying I have to make a speech?" Nikora frowned.

"Yes," Kai replied. "There will be many speeches but there should be plenty of beer and whisky to keep you occupied. This wedding will be low-key, but I have been to some weddings you wouldn't believe. I sing in English and Arabic and so my band and I are in great demand."

"You have really adapted to Egypt," smiled Nikora.

"Yes, uncle. Nikau had told me about this place but I wanted to see it for myself and I'm so glad I came. I can't thank Jeff enough. He has given me a trade but also an unbelievable experience. Tomorrow, we'll go to the military cemetery. I can't go there without crying. Such a waste."

Nikau, Kai, Nikora and Aroha went to the cemetery early in the morning. This was such a peaceful and very well-kept place. Nikora was taken aback by the sheer number of graves. White crosses were being dusted by several locals. Aroha thought this a peaceful but horrific place. Nikau directed them to the New Zealand section and Aroha felt weak at the knees. Nikora felt a knot in his stomach and suddenly started to sweat. They found the Maori graves and Aroha gave a long speech in which she said she would find their relatives. She would let them know they were being taken care of, all said through tears. Everyone had tears in their eyes. Aroha made them look at all the New Zealand graves. They found one man from Dunedin and Aroha gave another speech in English, he was a neighbour.

Nikora was glad to get back to the compound and the land of the living. Aroha was making plans for when they went back to New Zealand. Kai was with them; Nikau had gone back to work.

"Jeff was here at the same time these men were being killed. I cannot imagine what it was like. I must talk to him about that time. I respect him so much for giving Nikau and me a job and a chance to see another world."

"Yes, Kai. Your parents will be so proud of you, as your aunt and I are proud of you."

The low-key wedding was anything but. Nikora and Aroha had met Anna's parents and Nikora was informed by his wife that Anna's mother was the source of her beauty. Nikau had a new suit and looked so smart. Kai was more casually dressed but he also looked smart. This was a very large church and Nikora was marvelling at the architecture. When Anna entered the church on her father's arm, Aroha took a deep breath and muttered that this was real beauty. The service was very long and Nikora wondered how long he could stand. At the end, there was no opportunity for the bride and groom kiss as they were all whisked into the vestry to sign the register. After signing, Nikora and Aroha witnessed the kiss and Aroha broke down in tears. She had held the tears back during the ceremony but now she had to let go. There were plenty of photos and Hashim promised they would get an album before they went home. The reception had so much food that Nikora asked Hashim why.

"I'm transporting food every day," he replied, "and this is showing my trade. I have a surprise for you… Come with me and meet the New Zealand Ambassador and the Australian Consul."

"I'm so proud to see New Zealanders making their mark in Egypt and I'm particularly pleased you are Maoris," said the New Zealand Ambassador

"Thank you, sirs, for coming to our son's wedding. This is a big surprise — we are honoured." said Nikora.

These two diplomats had been in Egypt since the war, they obviously knew Hashim. Talking with Nikora and Ahora they had a long discussion about New Zealand and particularly the South Island. The Australian Consul had relatives in the South Island so he knew the place well. After about twenty minutes, Kai came to drag them away as the speeches were about to begin. They excused themselves and went back to the top table. Aroha was saying that it was unbelievable, she had never met such polite and knowledgeable gentlemen. Nikora was overwhelmed but now he had to remember his speech.

His speech went very well, he thanked Hashim for his hospitality. When he said that his son had married the most beautiful girl in Egypt, there were cheers. They did not understand Kai's speech in Arabic but there was lots of clapping and laughter.

Kai and his band came later in the evening, after an Egyptian orchestra had entertained until nearly midnight. Nikau and Anna had left before midnight to go to Alexandria for their honeymoon. Aroha made Nikau promise to have a wedding in New Zealand and Anna said she would love to see Nikau's home. After they left, Aroha said that they had to fix up their place.

Nikora and his wife had many sights to see before they joined their liner for the trip home. The farewell was large, with the whole family coming to the dockside. Nikora thanked Hashim and said he could never repay him for such a wonderful time. Hashim told him that just sending his son and nephew was thanks two-fold. Kai sang a hymn in the Maori language, which brought both Aroha and Nikora to tears. As the liner left the dock, there was lots of waving and cheers. Nikora said that the other passengers must think them special.

In New Zealand, the girls had gone back to university and Jeff was doing work in both garages. They were missing Nikau and Kai. One of the mechanics suggested they hire another young lad. Jeff was missing his recruiter, Nikora, so he asked the mechanic to look around and hire a helper.

Jeff had not visited the garage for a few weeks and when he did so, he saw a young man outside, smoking. He asked the lad if he worked in the garage.

"Only when I have to."

"Sorry, son. You're sacked. I'm the owner."

Jeff took the mechanic aside and told him what he had done and that he would find another more deserving lad. Gladys was very happy when he told her what he had done. She hoped the lad had learned a lesson and his next employer would reap the benefit.

News from the girls was all good and Gladys said they should visit Christchurch and have a short holiday in a hotel. Jeff thought the girls might think they were spying on them but Gladys said there was no need to contact them. Jeff couldn't do that and said they should forewarn them. Gladys smiled to herself, Jeff was such a straight fellow.

Christchurch was a very English city with parks and a small river, where people were punting. It reminded Jeff of Worcester, and Reggie and Sophie. They took the train across the Southern Alps to Greymouth. Neither of them had been on a train for many years and although it was cold, they spent most of the ride hanging off the back of one of the carriages. Greymouth was a small town with not much to see but this was the wild West Coast and the sea was in full force. The ride back was relaxing as they sat inside and met a couple from Brisbane. There was a lot of discussion of the merits of Australia versus New Zealand. Gladys asked Jeff about Brisbane. He said he preferred Dunedin as the weather was much cooler and more like England. Doing a manual job, Brisbane could be too hot and sticky and that was tiring.

"How about Egypt? Is it not hot there?"

"Yes, the first few days were torture. But it has a dry heat, particularly in the desert. I was younger then and like Nikau, I quickly adapted. I must take you there as soon as we save enough money. And we must also visit England."

"Oh, yes please," Gladys agreed. "I still have distant relatives there."

They did meet up with the girls for a dinner in a good restaurant, although the menu was dominated by fish dishes and plenty of chips with all them. Margaret did more talking than Julie, Gladys was surprised. Jeff asked Julie if anything was the matter. Julie answered that she had a new history course and she thought the lecturer had some problems with the World War. She was trying to make a case to refute some of his ideas. Later, Jeff said to Gladys that his daughter had become a real academic. Margaret said she would finish her degree and then go to England. Julie was going to take a Law course, and go to England with Margaret, she did not want her to get lost.

"Our daughters have a bond that you might expect of natural sisters," noted Jeff.

"I think there are other bonds, as yet a secret. Julie might tell you but Margaret is more secretive."

"I'm not sure what you mean but it might be female intuition and I won't go there."

Nikora and Aroha were back and invited Jeff and Gladys for a barbecue. Initially, Aroha did all the talking. Jeff had rarely spoken to her and Gladys had only seen Aroha a couple of times. Aroha was excitedly telling them about their trip and then she became serious. She started talking about the war graves and asked Jeff what it was like during the war.

"I saw very little fighting," Jeff admitted, "as we were a transport section. Our convoy did get strafed by Stukas and we had several dead. We had to cover them with sand and mark them so we could take them back to base when we returned. When I left, there were crews going out into the desert to bring the bodies back to Cairo."

After that, Aroha fell silent. Nikora now spoke about Nikau and Kai. Kai was the big surprise, he knew a lot of Arabic and even sang in Arabic with his band. Nikau's workshop was orderly and as clean as any workshop could be. Nikora added that Hashim was a great host and surprised them with a couple of guests at the wedding. Aroha interjected.

"To our surprise, we met the New Zealand Ambassador and the Australian Consul. Those two gentlemen made me proud they were representing us in Egypt. They were so intelligent and told us many stories. I could have listened to them all night."

"Hashim has lots of contacts and I'm sure he invited them. Did you meet a man we call the Quartermaster?" Jeff enquired.

"No, Hashim explained he was on leave in England," Nikora said.

The barbecue was a success and Aroha said Gladys must visit Cairo as it was such a magical place. When Jeff next saw Nikora, in the pub, they talked about Nikau and Anna. The girls had told Jeff she was beautiful.

"She is small but with a perfect figure, her skin is so clear and she has very dark eyes. I'm not a man who looks much at other women but it is hard not to look at her. Aroha thinks she is a beauty so I have confirmation. Aroha is in Wellington looking up military records, she

258

has this obsession with finding relatives of those two dead Maoris. She has photos of their graves and she wants to tell them about the cemetery. It's important to us to know where our brothers lie. She has contacted the family of the fellow from Dunedin and given them a photo. They were very pleased and I think we have made new friends."

A year went by and Julie graduated with first-class honours and entered a Law course. Margaret started the final year of her course. Jeff and Gladys visited Christchurch quite often, Gladys was sensing Jeff wanted to see Julie as often as he could. The news from Cairo was good with the happy information that Nikau and Anna were enjoying married life and that Anna might be expecting. Kai was to return to New Zealand shortly. Reggie and Sophie and their daughter had a short holiday in Egypt and were looking forward to seeing the girls next year. Reggie wrote to Jeff and told him how pleased he was to meet Nikau and Kai, and that Jeff had trained two very good mechanics, counting Hashim, he had trained three. Nabil and Tania had hit it off and Tania was fascinated with all the children in the compound. She was also enthralled by how different life was to that in England.

Kai arrived to a great reception. He warned he wasn't staying long but wanted to learn more of his language so he could write some songs in his language. His parents, aunt and uncle were so proud of him. He had been invited to the New Zealand Embassy for a big function and they had asked whether he could sing a Maori song and all he could think of was a couple of hymns. He wanted to listen to some local Maori songs. He had visited another couple of Commonwealth War Cemeteries and brought his aunt photos of Maori graves. He learned there were several grave sites. Ahora was overwhelmed; she kissed and hugged him while shedding plenty of tears. His parents were astounded with the change in their son and when he told them about the cemeteries, they were in tears. Nikau was preparing to come to New Zealand but now Anna was pregnant and the trip would be delayed. Kai told Jeff of his meeting with Reggie and Sophie. He said they were people of the highest class and they had invited him to stay with them if he ever journeyed to England.

Aroha now had a new task, to find relatives of the fallen. Nikora thought the news of a grandchild would be forefront in her mind. She explained that she knew it would happen but these photos were a real surprise. She had traced the families of the first two soldiers and now she was in contact with several families. Kai had listed the names and the dates they fell and the locations of their graves; he was such a considerate person. Kai went with Aroha to Wellington to listen to some local music. They then went to Auckland to find relatives and listen to music.

Kai returned before Aroha and visited Jeff in the garage.

"Jeff, I can never repay you for what you have done for me," he began. "You gave me a trade and then you sent me to Egypt to get experience. As soon as I arrived, I realised that I would be working with Egyptians whose English might be poor. I had to learn their language and try to understand their culture. It dawned on me that I did not know too much about my culture. That opened my eyes and really that is the greatest experience Egypt has given me."

Jeff smiled. "I hoped, by sending you to Egypt, you would learn to work under different conditions with different people. I can see more than that happened. I have lost a mechanic and gained a mature friend."

"You were there during the war," Kai continued. "What was it like? Those visits to the graves have had a serious effect on me."

"The real action I saw was at Dunkirk and I was so scared I jumped on a fishing boat to get away," admitted Jeff. "When we landed in England, I thought that the captain going back for more soldiers must be mad. In Egypt, my job was fixing old lorries to take supplies to the troops on the front line. I believe Hashim still has a couple of those lorries. I did see a bit of action and I was hiding under one of those old beasts. If you want to know more about the action, ask Major Ralph."

"I didn't know you were at Dunkirk, but I do know those old lorries. Fixing them in the desert must have been a real challenge. Fixing them in the workshop is a challenge. Hashim has told me some stories but the proudest moment was when you called him son," smiled Kai.

"Hashim was a good kid," Jeff confirmed. "And if he wasn't a Copt, he would have a place in the government. But we can't change our birth."

Kai told Jeff he would stay in Cairo for many years but he had not yet told his parents. Jeff's advice was to go back, write regularly to his parents and, if he earned enough money, to pay for them to come and visit. Kai was happy with that advice.

At their weekly pub meeting, Jeff told Nikora what Kai had said but not to tell his parents. Nikora had suspected Kai would go back and stay; Kai's father suspected the same. Nikora and Jeff both admitted that Kai was a revelation.

Kai returned to Egypt and later Nikora and Anna had a son. Aroha said that they now had both a wedding and a christening in the future. Photos of the baby and parents came in the mail, and Aroha showed them to everyone. Nikora took one to the pub, principally to show Anna to Jeff.

Part 8

Margaret's graduation was attended by Jeff, Julie and Gladys, who was so proud of her daughter. When she went to the stage to receive her certificate for a first-class honour, Julie rose to her feet and was clapping like mad. Jeff and Gladys were clapping but Julie's enthusiasm shocked them both. There was a reception in the Great Hall and Margaret was surrounded by well-wishers. Julie was standing with her father and stepmother when a man came over to talk to Jeff.

"I teach history and last year your daughter was a challenge. She told me you were at Dunkirk. What do you think of war?"

"War is madness, and should be avoided if possible," Jeff readily replied.

"I might use that in one of my lectures. Thank you for being so succinct."

Gladys turned to Jeff. "Keep this up and you'll be quoted in the whole of New Zealand."

"I know you are being sarcastic but I forgive you," he responded. Now they all laughed.

Later in the evening, they had a drink in a local pub by the cathedral. Julie and Margaret explained that they would go directly to England and not stop in Cairo.

Gladys whispered that they seemed anxious to get to England, but Jeff thought nothing of it. He told them he would give them time to settle in and then he and Gladys would visit England. On the way, they had to stop off in Cairo so Gladys could see something new, and of course to visit Hashim and his family. He was also interested to see how Nikau and Kai were coping.

A couple of months passed and the girls had jobs in Worcester. Julie was in a solicitor's office and Margaret was working for a seed company. Julie asked that they delay their visit to England as there might be a development later in the year. Jeff thought nothing of the request but Gladys was suspicious, there was something a foot. On one of their visits to Wellington, she had a long chat with Constance and they both thought romance had a lot to do with the delay.

Later in the year, Jeff received startling news. Julie and Margaret were each to be married to Ralph's sons. Margaret was to marry the younger son and Julie to marry the elder. Jeff was shocked but Gladys had a broad smile. She quickly phoned Constance to relay the news. They were both very excited.

Now Jeff had to plan their trip and Constance wanted to come. Harold would probably not make the journey, as there might be a General Election when they planned to travel. Jeff warned Hashim they would be three. Hashim's reply was to bring the whole family. Reggie and Sophie were so excited and they could easily house several visitors. Ralph and Gwen could do nothing but talk about the coming weddings.

Constance had not been back to England for many years, yet still had friends in Birmingham. She had never visited Cairo and being an avid reader of history, she was very keen to see the real thing. Gladys had a quiet cry about her little shy daughter being married, but she couldn't wait to board that liner.

As they landed in Cairo, they were welcomed by Hashim in a limousine.

"Have you borrowed this monster?" asked Jeff.

"I have a large family," answered Hashim, "and they do not like to travel in lorries."

Jeff introduced his wife and sister and Hashim kissed their hands. He opened the back door and offered them the back seat; Jeff was to sit in the front seat. Jeff noticed a few differences since he was in Cairo. Hashim's compound was impressive.

"How did you get all this land?" he marvelled.

"I bought out all my neighbours."

The welcome was rather overwhelming for Constance and Gladys. There was a lot of ululating and bowing. Hashim introduced his wife and son Nabil and apologised for his daughter, Asha, who was very shy. Nikau and Anna had been hiding in the crowd and they stepped forward, then there were hugs all around. Everything went quiet and from the back a lone voice started to sing. It was Kai singing a Maori hymn.

Constance was surprised, she had heard this hymn before and it bought tears to her eyes.

Jeff and the two ladies were escorted to the guest house and their luggage was bought to them. Jeff reached into his pocket but Hashim said there was no backsheesh in his compound. Gladys asked about backsheesh and Jeff explained it was a tip. There was little or no tipping in New Zealand or Australia, but Jeff explained that some people had such low salaries, they survived on backsheesh.

Hashim said that this evening there would be a feast at dusk. Jeff explained to the ladies that as it could get quite cool when the sun went down, they might need a shawl or jacket. He also told them there might be some dishes they were not used to, but to try everything. Gladys was laughing at her husband telling her what to eat.

Nikora had asked why there was so much food and Jeff said the same. The ladies were trying everything and Jeff felt silly telling them what to do. There was plenty to drink but the ladies only had a couple of glasses of wine. They noticed the other ladies drank nothing alcoholic.

The next day, the ladies were picked up by Kai and taken on a tour of the Pyramids and the Sphinx, while Jeff went to Nikau's workshop, which was very impressive. That evening they all met the Quartermaster in a very expensive hotel. Kai was present and said grace in his language. Kai and the Quartermaster were good friends and if there were customers to impress, Kai would sing in Arabic and then in Maori, that generally worked.

Gladys and Constance were very impressed with the hotel, the service and the food. Jeff told them he liked the local food better but he was just an ordinary man. Hashim laughed and said he was an extraordinary man. Hashim announced that, as his wife was pregnant, he was taking Kai to England and he would sing at the wedding. Kai was very happy.

"I loved Reggie and Sophie. I'm so keen to visit England and they invited me when they came here. I'm so excited to sing in an English church and your daughters are my sisters."

That bought a tear to Gladys's eye.

The ladies spent the next day in the compound, talking to the women and children. Jeff was busy going with Hashim to a meeting with local merchants. Hashim introduced Jeff as his mentor, who had been at Dunkirk. Suddenly the mood of the audience changed and Jeff was made to feel very welcome. One military man was present and when Jeff told of his service in Egypt, he was kissed on both cheeks.

Hashim took them to the museum the next day, and told them to ignore the guards, they would be rewarded later. Constance was enthralled by the exhibits and asked if she could come again and spend more time viewing them. Hashim said he would arrange for his cousin to take her the next day. Gladys wanted to see the scrap market and the desert, where Jeff had been stationed.

"I can take you into the desert but where we were stationed is a military zone. The market is rough but they all know me there and we'll be welcome."

The trip to the desert was a revelation to the ladies. They were not far from the Nile and the whole area was sand, with very little vegetation. The market was quite fun, they were greeted like royalty. When Jeff was introduced, one man reminded him that they did not get many *Khawajas* ('lords' or 'masters') visiting this market.

The next few days were spent relaxing, mainly in the compound, and the ladies became acquainted with the mothers and children. Nabil wasn't too happy, he wanted to marry Julie but if Margaret was available, he would marry her. Constance and Gladys had a good laugh after he left. Constance said those two girls made an impression wherever they went.

Kai had to show them the cemetery and the New Zealand part. At the Maori grave, he recited a short prayer, explaining that he couldn't come to this place without a prayer or a song. The cleaners all knew him and he had explained to them what he was doing. They all bowed when he came and left. He felt a bit embarrassed but he wouldn't tell them to stop. Constance and Gladys both expressed that this young man was a credit to his tribe and to New Zealand.

The leaving party was very special as Kai arrived with his band and sang all night. The ladies finally had an extensive conversation with Anna and both agreed she was very beautiful. She was preparing to visit her in-laws in New Zealand.

Jeff and the ladies were picked up at Heathrow by Reggie, who was in a very excited mood.

"Your daughters have turned my house upside down," he mock-complained. "There are so many women around, I'm completely outnumbered. I never really knew my nephews before but they are like extra lodgers. My daughter and Sophie are so happy, I can never have a serious conversation, it always ends in laughter. I think Ralph and Gwen are in another world, everything is about the wedding. We'll go to Ralph's place where there is a reception committee. Tomorrow, I'll go to Heathrow again, to pick up Hashim and Kai. In a way, I'm glad to be out of the madness."

Ralph's farm was decked out as though a coronation was taking place, and as they drove through the gates, there was a line up. Gladys had eyes only for Margaret and she looked so happy. Margaret introduced her future husband, Mark, after a long hug from her mother. Julie introduced her future husband, Riley, to Jeff and Constance. Then it was mayhem as everyone seemed to be talking at the same time. Gladys and Constance were introduced to Ralph and Gwen. Jeff introduced his wife and sister to Sophie and Tania and the mayhem continued. Gwen had set out a table of food in one of the barns as the numbers were so large. She indicated that there was no seating order and everyone could sit wherever they wished. This was a great party.

The girls would be staying at Ralph's place and Jeff, Gladys and Constance would stay at Reggie's house, where there would also be room for Hashim and Kai. The next day, while Reggie went to Heathrow, Jeff and Constance went to hire two cars. Constance wanted to visit Birmingham to visit some old friends and Jeff wanted to visit some of Gladys's relatives in Chester. Gladys was keen for Margaret to visit distant relatives and she also wanted to get her on her own. Jeff told Julie they would have a talk when he returned.

Constance visited some old friends who were surprised to see her, and she also caught up on all the gossip. Doreen was still alone and seemed resigned to living on her own. Gladys visited second cousins and they were all happy to see her and Margaret. Actually, though, Gladys was more interested in talking with her daughter.

She discovered that, on the first trip, Margaret had stayed with Ralph and Gwen, working on the farm. Ralph's sons were a bit shy at first. Mark was more interested in agriculture but Riley wanted to do something different. They went out as a foursome and suddenly, Julie took more interest in Riley. He wanted to travel and wasn't so interested in the farm. It seemed that the couples were matched, so they decided to have a double wedding. When they told Ralph and Gwen, they thought Gwen might have a heart attack, she was so pleased. Margaret loved the area and was planning to stay for many years.

Arriving back at Reggie's place at about the same time as Constance, they were greeted by a very excited Kai. It had been his first time on an aeroplane and he was very scared when they landed. He admitted he closed his eyes and had a little prayer. He was marvelling at Reggie's house and Tania had been showing him around the grounds. Constance smiled at the way Tania was looking at Kai. The next morning, Constance arose early, and when she looked out of the window, she saw Kai and Tania gambolling on the grass. She went outside.

"Kai — what are you doing?"

"Enjoying ourselves! I have lived in the desert a long time; I can't get over how green everything is and the feeling of this grass is magical. Later, I'm going with Tania to her school and I'll sing a hymn at their assembly. Sophie has fixed it with the headmistress. I'll also tell them about our culture. After the wedding, Hashim and I are going to London to see another side of England."

Constance smiled, the other side of England was in London. Obviously, Tania had talked her mother into this so she could show off her gorgeous visitor. Both Kai and Sophie had been very taken by Tania. Tania was another Julie.

Constance and Gladys went to see Gwen to talk about the wedding.

"I had two boys and when I met Julie I wanted a daughter," Gwen admitted. "Now I have two and one is Julie. I couldn't be happier and the couples suit each other. Mark is the quiet one, like Margaret; they both like the country life. Riley is more outgoing, like Julie, and they want to travel. I sensed the excitement in the boys when the girls arrived but when they said they would have a double wedding, it knocked me for six. Ralph does not say much but he is very happy and Jeff is the one who brought everyone together. He still talks about Jeff fixing his two tractors and now he has made friends with Arnold and sees his brother more often."

"Yes, Jeff is very special," Gladys agreed. "Before he came into my life," I was mourning a dead husband and had a very shy daughter. The change in my daughter was the most startling but I also appreciate the change in me."

"Looks like my brother is a miracle maker," laughed Constance, "but don't tell him."

A double wedding in Worcester was big news, two sisters marrying two brothers even reached the Birmingham Mail. Doreen read the names and saw her daughter was getting married; she would go to the wedding, come what may.

The big day arrived and the church was nearly full, as Jeff strode down the aisle with his two daughters on his arm. Gladys had told Constance that she would love to have taken Margaret down the aisle, but Jeff was doing a good job. Constance informed Gladys that as they entered the church, she had seen someone she knew. It was Doreen, who was sitting in the last row on the brides' side.

"Should I thank her for coming?" whispered Gladys.

"No, that might be embarrassing for my brother. Let him enjoy his big day."

Kai sang his hymn and started both Constance and Gladys crying. The audience stood in silence, then clapped when he explained what it meant.

There were lots of photographs; everyone seemed to have a camera. Constance scanned the crowd but couldn't see Doreen, and in a way, she was relieved.

The reception was held at Ralph's farm and luckily it was a fine day, as most activity occurred outside. It was a raucous affair with a band and plenty of dancing. The married couples left early, they were driving to London, staying a few days and would then go to France for their honeymoons.

Margaret said to her mother that she would introduce Mark to her biological father but Jeff was the best substitute. She and Mark would try to buy a house or smallholding in the Worcester area. She might not visit New Zealand for many years but she would, one day.

Julie told her dad and Constance that she and Riley would work for a year or two to earn some money. They would then visit Cairo, New Zealand and Australia. She wanted to show Riley where she had lived and he was keen to travel. Finally, she wanted to go to Sydney. All she could remember was the bridge but she had heard they were constructing a new type of Opera House and she wanted to see what it looked like.